Activate!

Music, Movement & More!

Mission Statement

Heritage Music Press and High/Scope Educational Research Foundation are proud to present this resource for all involved in teaching elementary students. We believe that music and movement are essential tools for learning and student achievement. It is our goal to present quality content that is developmentally appropriate, practical, and educationally sound. We strive to provide you with enjoyable opportunities to engage students in active learning.

Heritage Music Press

Heritage Music Press, a Lorenz Company, is dedicated to publishing the best in choral, classroom and instrumental music. Reaching students in kindergarten through high school, our music and resources are well crafted, accessible, age appropriate, educationally sound, and diverse in scope.

The Heritage Editorial Team
Blair Bielawski, JazzWorks and Instrumental music
Kris Kropff, Classroom resources
Lynne Latham, Latham Music and String music
Mary Lynn Lightfoot, Choral music

The Lorenz Corporation
Geoffrey R. Lorenz, Chairman
Reiff Lorenz, President
Larry F. Pugh, President, Music Publishing
Barbara Meeks, Vice President, Marketing

High/Scope Educational Research Foundation

The High/Scope Foundation is an independent nonprofit research, development, training, and public advocacy organization with headquarters in Ypsilanti, Michigan. High/Scope's mission is to lift lives through education by engaging in curriculum development, research, training, and publishing and communication.

Larry Schweinhart, President
Movement and Music Division
Karen S. Sawyers, Director
Phyllis S. Weikart, Senior Advisor
Nancy Brickman, Director of Publications

High/Scope Educational Research Foundation
600 North River Street
Ypsilanti, MI 48198-2898
734/485-2000
www.highscope.org

HERITAGE MUSIC PRESS
Diverse Resources for *Your* Music Classroom
a Lorenz company • www.lorenz.com

HIGH/SCOPE®
Educational Research Foundation

From the Editor

Greetings and Happy Holidays!

In spite of the fact that last January I once again said to myself, "Never again! Next year, I'm getting my holiday act together," the holidays have arrived and my act is far from together. I find myself going in at least ten different directions, and the idea of pulling any of them into a single and concise narrative thread is enough to send me running for the spiked apple cider. Hence, I offer these bullet points from the editor. (If you're one of those people that finished your Christmas shopping in July and had all of your holiday meals planned months ago, please forgive me. For everyone else, I'm sure you understand, and appreciate the brevity!)

- **Welcome, Patty Bourne!** I am delighted to announce that Patty Bourne, a veteran music educator and master teacher from the Seattle area, is taking us *Inside the Music Classroom* in her new regular column. A recent addition to the Heritage Music Press team, Patty will also be authoring lesson plans to complement the songs and activities in *Activate!* and will be serving as a valued editorial consultant as well.
- **Mixed Media CD.** Because we're continuing to include more and more additional content on the CD (and this issue is no exception), we've expanded the contents to three pages and are now listing both the audio and data files on page 7. A sneak peek: we're including files for all the lyric sheets so you can project them—no typing required.
- **Come say hello.** Starting in January, Heritage Music Press will be out and about on the convention trail. For those of you attending the MEA convention in Florida, Texas or Ohio, please stop by our booth in the exhibition hall and say hello! Convention details are on our Web site, www.lorenz.com. Also there is information about the workshops and clinics our many fantastic contributors are presenting around the country.
- **Share a laugh.** If you're like me, getting back into gear after the holidays can be challenging. Sometimes the only thing that will do the trick is a good laugh. To that end, I offer a few student one-liners that have been passed around over the years. If your students have been the inadvertent source of a similar laugh, or if you have a funny story that your fellow educators would appreciate, please send it to me at activate@lorenz.com. It would be great to include them in a future issue.

  "Handel was half German, half Italian and half English; he was rather large."

  "I like to listen to the Sorcerer's Appendix."

  "Felix Mendelssohn seems to have been happy, honest and well-liked, although a musician."

  "A diminuendo is something only encyclopedias know for sure."

Hope your New Year gets off to a wonderful start, and I'll talk to you again in February, when children's literature in the music classroom will be our focus.

Kris Kropff
Editor

Statement of Ownership, Management and Circulation
(Required by 39 U. S. C. 3685)

1. Publication Title: Activate!
2. Publication Number: 1931-4736
3. Filing Date: September 28, 2007
4. Issue Frequency: Bi-monthly, except June and July
5. Number of Issues Published Annually: 5
6. Annual Subscription Price: $64.95
7. Office of Publication *(Not printer)*: 501 E. Third St., P.O. Box 802, Dayton, Montgomery County, OH 45401–0802, U.S.A.
8. General Business Office *(Not printer)*: 501 E. Third St., P.O. Box 802, Dayton, Montgomery County, OH 45401–0802, U.S.A.
9. Publisher: Lorenz Publishing Co., 501 E. Third St., P.O. Box 802, Dayton, Montgomery County, OH 45401–0802, U.S.A.
   Editor: Kris Kropff, 501 E. Third St., P.O. Box 802, Dayton, Montgomery County, OH 45401–0802, U.S.A.
   Managing Editor: Larry Pugh, 501 E. Third St., P.O. Box 802, Dayton, Montgomery County, OH 45401–0802, U.S.A.
10. Owner: Heritage Music Press, a division of The Lorenz Corporation, Reiff Lorenz, President, 501 E. Third St., P.O. Box 802, Dayton, Montgomery County, OH 45401–0802, U.S.A.
11. Bondholders: None
13. Activate!
14. Issue Date for Circulation Data Below: August/September 2007
15. Extent and Nature of Circulation

	Average No. Copies Each Issue During Preceding 12 months	No. Copies of Single Issue Published Nearest to Filing Date
a. Total Number of Copies *(Net press run)*	4,037	3,715
b. Paid and/or Requested Circulation		
1. Paid/Requested Outside-County Mail Subscriptions Stated on Form 3541	2,772	2,068
2. Paid In-Country Subscriptions Stated on Form 3541	10	6
3. Sales Through Dealers and Carriers, Street Venders, Counter Sales, and Other Non-USPS Paid Distribution	732	1,350
4. Other Classes Mailed Through the USPS	57	84
c. Total Paid and/or Requested Circulation *[Sum of 15b. (1), (2), (3), and (4)]*	3,571	3,508
d. Free Distribution by Mail *(Samples, complimentary, and other free)*		
1. Outside-County as Stated on Form 3541	0	0
2. In-County as Stated on Form 3541	0	0
3. Other Classes Mailed Through the USPS	0	0
4. Free Distribution Outside the Mail *(Carriers or other means)*	72	67
e. Total Free Distribution *(Sum of 15d. and 15e.)*	72	67
f. Total Distribution (sum of 15c. & 15f.)	3,643	3,575
g. Copies not Distributed	308	87
h. Total (sum of 15g. & h.)	3,951	3,662
i. Percent Paid and/or Requested Circulation *(15c. divided by 15g. times 100)*	98%	98%

16. Publication of Statement of Ownership will be printed in the December 2007/January 2008 issue of this publication.
17. Signature and Title of Editor, Publisher, Business Manager, or Owner
    Date: September 28, 2007

I certify that all information furnished on this form is true and complete. I understand that anyone who furnishes false or misleading information on this form or who omits material or information requested on the form may be subject to criminal sanctions (including fines and imprisonment) and/or civil sanctions (including civil penalties).

Reiff Lorenz, President

Contributors

Patricia Bourne teaches K–6 general music, 5th/6th-grade chorus, and a 6th-grade marimba ensemble at Canyon Creek Elementary in Bothell, WA. A frequent guest conductor and clinician, she has severed on the editorial committee of *General Music Today* and recently authored *Inside the Music Classroom: Teaching the Art with Heart.* Patty received her B.M.E. from Murray State University, M.M.E. from University of Oklahoma, and Doctorate of Education from Arizona State University.

Beth Bryant is a music educator with 24 years of teaching experience in central and western Massachusetts. She is currently teaching K–5 music at Corley Elementary School in Lawrenceville, Georgia. Beth has taught both vocal and instrumental music in preschool- through college-level classrooms and is a field consultant for the Movement and Music Division of High/Scope.

Mark Burrows has written music and curriculum for numerous major publishers. His song collections, including the *Gettin' Down with Mama Goose* series, top many best-seller lists. Known to many little listeners as "Mister Mark," he tours nationally, presenting high-energy family concerts. Mark received his undergraduate degree in music education from Southern Methodist University and his graduate degree in conducting from Texas Christian University.

Donna Dirksing is an elementary music teacher for the Forest Hills School District in Cincinnati, Ohio. She holds a B.A. in Music Education from Transylvania University and a M.M. in Music Education with a specialization in Orff-Schulwerk from the University of Cincinnati College-Conservatory of Music. Holding all three levels of Orff certification, Donna is a frequent presenter of workshops and clinics.

Jerry Estes currently teaches vocal music at Wydown Middle School for grades six through eight. He received his B.M.E. with a vocal emphasis from Southwest Baptist University and his M.M. from Southern Illinois University. Jerry and his wife, Julie, have two children, Haley and Baxter.

Linda Forrest has been an active composer, arranger and clinician for many years. Having earned her Bachelor of Music degree from Oklahoma City University and master's in Kodály Education from the University of Oklahoma, she also earned certification in all levels of Orff and Kodály. Linda is a member of American Orff-Schulwerk Association and Oklahoma Music Educators Association and has served as President of the Oklahoma Orff Chapter.

Denise Gagné has taught band, choir and classroom music from pre-school to college. Holding degrees in music and education, as well as certification in Kodály and Orff training, Denise is currently teaching part-time music, and conducts the Red Deer Children's Choir. Her choirs and bands have won many awards at music festivals and have performed for local and national sporting events, on national radio and even for the Queen. Denise has authored many elementary music publications including the *Musicplay K–6* textbook.

For nearly four decades **Terry Kirkland** worked to advance the repertoire and musicianship of children's choirs. After graduating from the University of Alabama, he joined the staff of the Baptist Sunday School Board as Children's Choir Specialist. After almost twenty years there, he became editor of Triune Music and ultimately founded Kirkland House, a publisher specializing in music for children's choir, including the curriculum series *I Like Music.*

Contributors (continued)

Mary Lynn Lightfoot is the Choral Editor for Heritage Music Press. A successful composer, she has over 200 titles in print and is in constant demand throughout the country as a clinician and guest conductor. Prior to helming HMP, Mary Lynn was an elementary general music and choral educator in her home state of Missouri.

Loretta Mitchell teaches elementary general and choral music and serves as the K–12 Music Coordinator. She is the author of numerous general music resources, including *One, Two, Three…Echo Me.* Loretta received her undergraduate degree from St. Olaf College and a Master of Science degree in Music Education from the University of Illinois at Urbana – Champaign.

Brad Printz began composing and arranging choral music in 1988 and built a catalog of nearly 50 pieces before succumbing to cancer in 2005 after a heroic 15-year struggle. Holding a B.M.E. and a B.M. in Theory/Composition, Brad was a music teacher at Piper Jr./Sr. High School in Kansas City, Kansas for ten years prior to serving as choral manager for J.W. Pepper at Wingert-Jones Music in Kansas City, Missouri.

Ruth Elaine Schram began composing as a child, and her first octavo was published in 1988. In 1992, she became a full-time arranger and composer and now has over 1,000 pieces in print. Her many works for choir reflect her gift for melody and message, yet remain practical and accessible, thanks, no doubt, to her early experiences teaching elementary music.

Phyllis S. Weikart is Senior Advisor to the Movement and Music Division of the High/Scope Educational Research Foundation. She conducts training workshops and conference sessions for music, physical education, and early childhood educators throughout the United States on the importance of developmentally appropriate methods for using the kinesthetic intelligence to support learning.

Activate!

Editor
Kris Kropff

Editorial Assistant
Bonnie J. Krueger

Design
Janine M. Chambers • Digital Dynamite, Inc.

Art Department
Brenda Knowis • Patti Jeffers • Jeff Richards

Music Engravers
Jeanette Dotson • Linda Taylor

Recording Producers
Blair Bielawski • Mark Burrows • Phyllis S. Weikart

Activate! (ISSN: 1931-4736) is a periodical published bimonthly except June and July by Heritage Music Press, a division of The Lorenz Corporation, 501 East Third St., P.O. Box 802, Dayton, OH 45401-0802. Periodicals postage paid at Dayton, OH 45401. **Prices**: $64.95 for an eight-month subscription (five issues); $124.95 for a two-year subscription (ten issues); $179.95 for a three-year subscription (fifteen issues). **Subscription prices include postage.** Please contact us for pricing for subscribers outside of the U.S. Individual issues are available for $19.95 each. Please notify *Activate!* and your postmaster when changing address. Allow four to six weeks for processing.

Postmaster: Please send address change to *Activate!*, P.O. Box 802, Dayton, OH 45401-0802.

To subscribe to *Activate!* or for other general inquiries, visit www.activatemagazine.com, call our customer service department at 800/444-1144 x1, or e-mail service@lorenz.com. Letters to the editor may be emailed to activate@lorenz.com or mailed to *Activate!* at P.O. Box 802, Dayton, OH 45401.

Contents

Ready, Set, Sing
Simple Songs and Activities

Ready, Set, Play
Songs to Utilize Classroom Instruments

Contents (continued)

Education Through Movement
Movement Activities and Teaching Strategies

The *Fun*damentals
Games and Activities to Teach Music Terms and Concepts

K-3

4-6

The Activate! CD

The CD included with this issue is a mixed-media CD. It can be played in your stereo or CD player just like any "regular" CD, but it also includes data files that you can access through your computer. You will need the free Adobe Acrobat Reader to open these files. You may download it from www.abode.com/downloads/. You'll find the Download link for Adobe Reader under "Players, readers and viewer." If you have any trouble accessing these files, please contact us at activate@lorenz.com.

All computers will behave differently depending on their individual settings. PC users who are *not* using iTunes as their default media player will likely get a pop-up with several options—in addition to Play/Import the CD using iTunes or Windows Media Player, there should also be an option to Open Folder to View Files. Selecting that option will display a list of all the files on the CD; you can open or print the pages you need from this list, or save them to your local drive. If using iTunes, the CD will likely open in that program and ask if you want to import the audio files. If that's the case and you're a PC user, to access the file list you'll need to open Windows Explorer and click on the CD drive under "My Computer." Mac users will likely get two CD icons on the desktop—one for the audio files and one for the data files. Clicking on the data files icon will display a list of the files on the CD.

Data Files

The following parts and reproducibles are included on the CD. Plus, we've included all of the lyric sheets as they appear in the issue so that you may project the page rather than making a copy for each student, if so desired.

Piano/Vocal scores for:
- *Cousin Buford*
- *Celebrate With Me*
- *Hurry, Santa!*
- *The Mountain*

For *We Wish You a Merry Christmas:*
- Opt. Piano Accompaniment
- Reproducible Instrument Parts
- Form Visual
- "Which Fits?" Reproducible

For *It's Kwanzaa, Let's Celebrate:*
- Opt. Piano Accompaniment
- Reproducible Instrument Parts
- Rhythm Flashcards (4)
- Xylophone Visual

CD Tracks

Here's an easy way to keep your Activate! CDs organized. Just photocopy and cut out this label and keep it with this issue's disc.

Activate! *December | 2007 January | 2008*
CD Tracks

Tap Your Shoulders
- 1. Performance (0:40)
- 2. Accompaniment (0:40)

3. Burnie Bee (1:57)

Cousin Buford
- 4. Performance (2:38)
- 5. Accompaniment (2:38)

Celebrate With Me
- 6. Performance (2:03)
- 7. Accompaniment (2:03)

Hurry, Santa!
- 8. Performance (1:44)
- 9. Accompaniment (1:44)

The Mountain
- 10. Performance (1:26)
- 11. Accompaniment (1:26)

Some Love Coffee
- 12. Performance (1:37)
- 13. Accompaniment (1:37)

Christmas Train
- 14. Performance (1:10)
- 15. Accompaniment (1:10)

We Wish You a Merry Christmas
- 16. As written (1:02)
- 17. Accomp. ♩ = 90 (1:05)
- 18. Accomp. ♩ = 98 (0:59)

It's Kwanzaa, Let's Celebrate!
- 19. As written 𝅗𝅥 = 70 (2:13)
- 20. As written 𝅗𝅥 =80 (1:56)
- 21. Accompaniment (1:56)

22. Alpha-Beat Soup Voiced (0:18)
23. Alpha-Beat Soup Unvoiced (0:19)
24. Beatboxing Sounds (1:23)
25–28. Beatboxing Solos
29. Group Beatbox (0:45)
30. How Doth the Little Crocodile (0:22)
31. Sellenger's Round (2:50)
32. Apat-Apat (2:21)
33. Mexican Mixer (2:06)

National Standards for Music Education Index

Is It Really "Fun"?

by Patricia Bourne

"Boy, are you going to have FUN today!," exclaimed the energetic teacher to the 5th graders as they walked into the music room. In an attempt to motivate the students to bound in with unabashed enthusiasm, she anxiously tried to appeal to their pre-disposed goal to experience "fun" (in anything and everything). Would it work? Was "fun" the right word to include in the greeting? Or would it backfire?

I wish I could only guess at the answers, but since I was the energetic teacher who uttered these words, I don't have to guess. I can tell you, no, it didn't work; no, "fun" wasn't the right word; and yes, it did backfire.

While I applaud the enthusiasm that leads teachers, myself included, to use a "fun" greeting, ultimately, I set up myself—not to mention the students—with a less-than-accurate depiction of what we'd accomplish in class. As a matter of fact, one surly alpha male responded to my opening statement by replying, "Why? We goin' outside or something?" That was how a "fun" lesson became a challenging one. Within the first five minutes, students were wondering, "So, when's the fun going to start?," and I was regretting my choice of words.

What was I thinking? While the intent was noble, the strategy was misinformed. I believe that we can construct our learning environments to encourage, welcome and invite happy, satisfied learners without describing it as "fun." That particular word generates multiple meanings—"fun" ensues on the playground; "fun" occurs at a great party. Fun is a loaded noun, "an activity that provides amusement" and "playful joking, often at the expense of another." Yikes!

Rather than refer to the fun we'd have, I could've said "I'm sure glad to see you." I could've conveyed how much their participation was valued. I could've allowed the lesson to unfold, engaging them in strategies, challenges and developmentally appropriate activities that lead them to think, "This is a good time. I'm really enjoying myself!"

What do we *really* want to occur when students are present in our classes? I believe general music teachers have the best interest of their students in mind—we want our lessons to be ones that offer optimal learning for whomever is in our presence. We want students to walk through our doors assuming they will learn. We switch gears every 30 to 40 minutes to accommodate multiple grade levels in a single day; more so, we create lessons that keep students focused. We work hard! Do we have "fun" in our profession? Sure...most of the time. Are we expected to provide a place where students *have fun*? No. We are not entertainers, even though we must often be entertaining. We are not comedians, even though we use humor to capture a student's attention. We are not responsible for a child's overall "jolly time," even though we repel teaching in a way that makes students miserable (thus, making *us* miserable!).

I thoroughly enjoy my profession, but I would not use the word "fun" to capture in a single word all that it involves. Is it fun? Yes, usually! But again, is that the word that sums it up? Probably not. Is that bad news? I think not! It means we consider our profession to be more than an entertaining center for a child's amusement. Should our classrooms provide opportunities for fun? Sure! As long as the long-term purpose is focused on motivating students to open their minds and hearts to what a quality music education has to offer.

As an alternative to the loaded noun "fun," let our classrooms be described as a place where joyful, fulfilling, satisfying, empowering, rewarding, enjoyable learning occurs. There is a difference, and one that makes all the difference inside your music classroom!

TAP YOUR SHOULDERS

by Terry Kirkland

Suggested Grades K–1

Concepts

Sol-do
Singing vs. speaking voice
High/low

Perf. 1 **Acc.** 2

Tap Your Shoulders is a great movement song for primary students.

Have the students sing and do what the lyrics say: Tap shoulders, touch knees, etc. They will enjoy learning to sing the song faster and faster, but they will also want to sing it louder and louder. Encourage them to sing the song, not shout it. A good rule to introduce is: The faster you go, the softer you sing.

This song also provides a good opportunity to remind the children of high and low sounds.

The CD tracks for *Tap Your Shoulders* include a 2-bar introduction. The song is then sung/played four times, with a faster tempo taken on each repeat.

TAP YOUR SHOULDERS

Terry Kirkland

Passing Games With Primary

by Denise Gagné

Suggested Grade Kindergarten	***Materials***
Concepts	Bumblebee (see note below)
Steady beat Head voice (opt.) Loud and soft (opt.)	**Perf.** 3

Passing games are an excellent way to reinforce beat. However, they don't work very well with kindergarten-aged children. You may have greater success choosing one child to be a "beat keeper." In this game, the beat keeper holds a bumblebee; you can use a stuffed bee, a bumblebee puppet, a bee fly swatter, or a picture of a bee. (The facing page is reproducible and includes two bumblebee pictures.)

Process

1. The children form a circle. The beat keeper (who is holding a bumblebee) walks around the inside of the circle and points to the children in the circle, one at a time, on each beat.
2. The children in the circle hold out their hands. As the children sing the first six measures of *Burnie Bee*, the beat keeper taps the hands of each child on the beat. On the first beat of the seventh measure, on the words "take your wings and fly away," the beat keeper gives the bumblebee to the child at which he or she is pointing. That child flies around the circle and back to his or her place.
3. A new child is made the beat keeper and the game continues.

Burnie Bee

Traditional

Expand It!

- If you can find two bumblebees in contrasting sizes, you can use the song to practice using head voice. The beat keeper holds the larger bee as all students sing the song in a low voice. The next time the song is sung, the beat keeper holds the smaller bee as all students sing the song in a high voice. Using a very low voice and then changing to a very high voice helps some children who are stuck in chest voice discover their head voice.

Loud and Soft

Use the following related chant, *Here Is a Beehive,* to experiment with loud and quiet voices. The children speak the chant several times, loud then quiet, or change dynamics on each phrase as indicated by the teacher. On "Buzz, buzz, buzz," students vary the pitch of their voices up and down. Corresponding movements are also suggested.

Here Is a Beehive

Here is the beehive.	*Show clenched fist*
Where are the bees?	*Shrug with palms up*
Hidden away were nobody sees	*Show clenched fist*
Watch and you will see them	
Come out of their hives:	
One, two, three, four, five.	*Bring out fingers quickly one by one*
Buzz, buzz, buzz.	*Hold thumb and pointer finger together and "fly" like a bee*

Holiday Rondo

by Loretta Mitchell

Suggested Grades 2–3

Concept

Form: Rondo

Materials

Holiday songs
Script for reader(s)
Mural

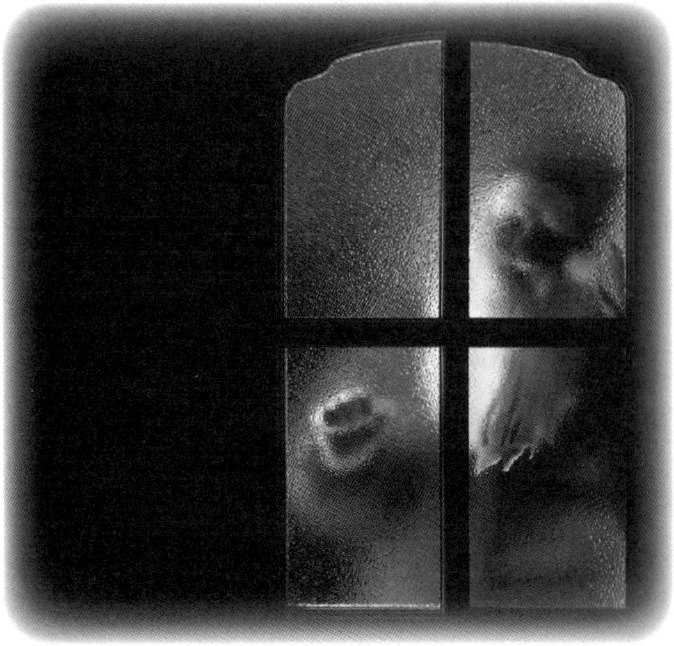

Holiday Rondo is a performance plan that features an original melody as the A part and uses familiar carols to create the rondo form (ABACADAEAF). It also includes an optional narrative script with a student-created holiday mural that teaches the audience about rondo form.

A suggested sequence of melodies to include in your *Holiday Rondo* is below. This performance plan allows students of every ability level to perform successfully. The entire class might learn the A part *(Holiday Rondo)* while small groups (or individual grades or classes) learn the other sections, according to their difficulty. Of course, you can modify this list, or expand the rondo to include other pieces your students are learning.

A	Holiday Rondo
B	Jingle Bells
C	Up on the Housetop
D	Jolly Old St. Nicholas
E	Good King Wenceslas
F	We Wish You a Merry Christmas

To perform *Holiday Rondo* using the narration found on the facing page, your students will need to create a mural. The mural should be a series of store windows, with each window representing one section of the rondo. The mural could be created on one long roll of paper, or each window could be on its own piece of poster board. Let your students decide on the theme of each window, perhaps making those students performing a particular section responsible for that window in the mural.

Once the windows have been designed, invite the students who created the murals for the A and B windows to write descriptions that will be used in the narration. You may elect to have one student read all of the narration or divide the reader parts among all several students.

This idea may also be adapted for use during seasons other than Christmas, for example *Halloween Rondo* or *Springtime Rondo.* [!]

Holiday Rondo

by Loretta Mitchell

Reader: Our class has created a rondo combining several familiar holiday melodies. Before we perform it for you, we'd like to take a few minutes to demonstrate how a rondo works.

Reader: Let's compare a rondo to a series of store windows. First we have a window containing ____. We call this window the A part.

Unroll mural to display Window A

Sing "Holiday Rondo"

Reader: We'll hear that tune many times during our rondo. Next, we will see a window decorated with ____. This is called the B part.

Unroll mural to display Window B

Sing "Jingle Bells"

Reader: We will bring back the A part at this point. It's just like seeing the ________________________ window again.

Sing "Holiday Rondo"

Reader: Now we need another new melody. We have chosen *Up on the Housetop.*

Unroll mural to display Window C

Sing "Up on the Housetop"

Reader: Again, the A part returns, followed by a new melody, the D part. The A part comes back after every new addition.

Reader: We'll perform the entire *Holiday Rondo* for you now without interruption. You might wish to follow our large musical map to keep track of the decorated store windows as you listen.

Get Set to Sing

A note from Kris Kropff, Editor

As I've mentioned before, we learned a lot from the survey we conducted at the end of last year, including the fact that the vast majority of you (and more importantly, your students) really enjoy our songs, and depend on them for PTA programs and other performances. We also discovered that many of you conduct an elementary choir and use some of the selections in *Activate!* to help round out your repertoire. While reading praise never gets old, I'm particularly appreciative of the constructive criticism we received, as it best highlights what we need to improve. Among the areas for improvement that were brought to our attention was the number of Christmas selections in the December/January issue; specifically, you wanted more of them.

In our ongoing efforts to do more of what you like and improve what you don't, this issue includes more songs than any of our previous seven, including a flexible performance plan by Loretta Mitchell, *Holiday Rondo,* and three choral pieces well suited to a variety of holiday concerts: play up the humorous *Cousin Buford*, by Brad Printz, with Western shirts and reindeer antlers; accent any winter concert with the rhythmic *Celebrate With Me*, by Jerry Estes; and hurry along the holidays with Ruth Elaine Schram's playful *Hurry, Santa!*. This issue also includes a concert piece for upper-elementary students. In *The Mountain*, the lush music of Mary Lynn Lightfoot sets off a text by the great American poet Emily Dickinson. Cross-curricular opportunities abound, in addition to the opportunities for musical growth.

To make room for all this great stuff, we've included the piano/vocal scores on the Mixed Media CD rather than printing them in the issue. As always, we've included the lyric sheets in the issue, but we've also put them on the CD so you can project the text without having to retype it. (See page 7 for information about the Mixed Media CD). Finally, on the subject of the CD, I would be remiss if I didn't thank Cathy Pfeiler and her great students at Arrowhead High School in Hartland, Wisconsin, for sharing their voices with us! (!)

Correction to *The Star-Spangled Banner*

The first "factoid," about the origins of Francis Scott Key's poem that became *The Star-Spangled Banner,* provided on page 13 of the October/November 2007 issue is incorrect. My apologies for the error. Accurate and expanded information about the origins of our national anthem follows. It is quoted from "The Story of the Flag" on the Smithsonian's National Museum of American History Web site *The Star-Spangled Banner: The Flag that Inspired the National Anthem.*

> On Sept. 14, 1814, Francis Scott Key peered through clearing smoke to see an enormous flag flying proudly after a 25-hour British bombardment of Baltimore's Fort McHenry. Key first published his impressions of the Fort McHenry victory as a broadside* poem, with a note that it should be sung to the popular British melody *To Anacreon in Heaven.*
>
> Francis Scott Key was a gifted amateur poet and hymnist. Inspired by the sight of the American flag flying over Fort McHenry the morning after the bombardment, he scribbled the initial notes for his poem on the back of a letter. Back in Baltimore, he copied the four verses onto paper, probably making more than one copy. The next morning someone printed the poem as a broadside.
>
> The melody to which Francis Scott Key intended his poem to be sung was the popular English tune known as *To Anacreon in Heaven.* Written about 1775 by John Stafford Smith, the tune was originally the "constitutional song" of the Anacreontic Society, a gentlemen's music club in London named after the 6th-century B.C.E. Greek poet Anacreon.

The first broadside was published under the header "Defence of Fort McHenry." The following was also added in introduction to Key's poem.

> The annexed song was composed under the following circumstances –
> A gentleman had left Baltimore, in a flag of truce for the purpose of getting released from the British fleet, a friend of his who had been captured at Marlborough.—He went as far as the mouth of the Patuxent, and was not permitted to return lest the intended attack on Baltimore should be disclosed. He was therefore brought up the Bay to the mouth of the Patapsco, where the flag vessel was kept under the guns of a frigate, and he was compelled to witness the bombardment of Fort McHenry, which the Admiral had boasted that he would carry in a few hours, and that the city must fall. He watched the flag at the Fort through the whole day with an anxiety that can be better felt than described, until the night prevented him from seeing it. In the night he watched the Bomb Shells, and at early dawn his eye was again greeted by the proudly waving flag of his country.

Facsimiles of this broadside as well as of the earliest known manuscript of Francis Scott Key's poem are available at the Smithsonian's impressive Web site, americanhistory.si.edu/ssb, along with additional articles, interactive "You Solve the Mystery" pages, and extensive educator information. (!)

* *From The Library of Congress:* Broadsides *are single sheets of paper, printed on one side only. Often quickly and crudely produced in large numbers and distributed free in town squares, taverns, and churches or sold by chapmen for a nominal charge, broadsides are intended to have an immediate popular impact and then to be thrown away.*

COUSIN BUFORD

Music by Brad Printz
Words by Ann Printz and Brad Printz

Did you know that Rudolph has a cousin from out West?
Ev'ry year he wants to be on Santa's team like all the rest.
But, Dasher, Dancer and the others always have to ride his case,
For ev'ry time they're in a hurry, guess who's movin' at a cowboy's pace!

Here comes Buford pokin' down the snowy trail.
Slowpoke Buford slower than a tired snail.
Come on Buford! Put a hitch in your git-a-long!
Can't you speed up? Can't we get you keyed up,
You tag-a-long?

Santa's got to get a move on 'cause it's Christmas Eve.
"Hitch the team!" he calls, and gives his bag of toys a heave!
"Your cousin needs to get in gear or things will get much worse!"
But, Santa doesn't know that his only gears are 'Park' and 'First'!

Here comes Buford pokin' down the snowy trail.
Slowpoke Buford slower than a tired snail.
Come on Buford! Put a hitch in your git-a-long!
Can't you speed up? Can't we get you keyed up,
You tag-a-long?

Stop your crawlin', a special load we're haulin'!
The kids will all be weepin' if their socks aren't heapin'!
Can't you keep up? Don't you fall asleep
or we'll be gone!

Spoken
Voice 1: C'mon, Buford!
Voice 2: Don't get left behind!
Voice 3: You're slowin' down even more, Buford!
Voice 4: C'mon!
All voices: Hurry, Buford! Git-a-long now!

Perf. 4 Acc. 5

COUSIN BUFORD

Words and Music by Brad Printz
Words by Ann Printz

*In the absence of temple blocks, use any low- and high-pitched, hollow-sounding percussion.

29
Come on Bu - ford! Put a hitch in your git - a - long!
33
Can't you speed up? Can't we get you keyed up, you
to Coda
37
tag - a - long? San - ta's got to
mf
42
get a move on 'cause it's Christ - mas Eve. "Hitch the team!" he
46
calls, and gives his bag of toys a heave! "Your cous - in needs to
50
get in gear or things will get much worse!" But, San - ta does - n't
54
molto rit.
D.S. al Coda
know that his on - ly gears are 'Park' and 'First'!

CODA
Stop your crawl - in', a spe - cial load we're haul - in'! The
kids will all be weep - in' if their socks aren't heap - in'!
Can't you keep up? Don't you fall a - sleep or
dim. poco a poco
we'll be gone!
Spoken: Voice 1
mf C'mon, Buford!
Voice 2
Don't get left behind!
pp
mf
Voice 3
You're slowin' down even more, Buford!
Voice 4
C'mon!
All voices
f Hur - ry, Bu - ford! Git - a - long now!

Celebrate With Me

Words and Music by Jerry Estes

This is the season we celebrate,
Friends and fam'lies from far and near.
Diff'rent people in diff'rent ways,
Spreading their good will and cheer.

So, come take my hand,
Together we will stand
and sing, sing in harmony.
No matter what the season, ev'rybody has a reason,
So celebrate, celebrate with me.

Some will hang colors of red and green,
Some tell stories of long ago.
Some will dance and some will sing,
Some will set candles aglow.

So, come take my hand,
Together we will stand
and sing, sing in harmony.
No matter what the season, ev'rybody has a reason,
So celebrate, celebrate with me.

So, come take my hand,
Together we will stand
and sing, sing in harmony.
No matter what the season, ev'rybody has a reason,
So celebrate, celebrate with me.

Celebrate, celebrate with me,
Celebrate, celebrate with me,
Celebrate, celebrate with me.

Celebrate With Me

Perf. 6 Acc. 7

Words and Music by
Jerry Estes

27
sing, sing in har - mo - ny. No mat-ter what the sea - son,
30
ev - 'ry - bod - y has a rea - son, so cel - e - brate, cel - e - brate with me.
33
Cel - e - brate, cel - e - brate with me, cel - e - brate, cel - e - brate with
36
rit.
me, cel - e - brate, cel - e - brate with me.

Hurry, Santa!

Words and Music by David Davenport and Ruth Elaine Schram

Hurry, Santa, Christmas is a-coming!
Time to make the Christmas toys.
Call the elves and get them all a-working,
Making gifts for girls and boys.

Prancer's dancing, Dancer is a-prancing,
Soon you'll hitch them to your sleigh.
Hurry, Santa, Christmas is a-coming!
Hurry up, Christmas Day!

Hurry, Santa, see the snow is falling,
Covering the frozen ground.
Donner and Blitzen's shoes, they need a-fixin',
So their hooves won't make a sound.

Roof to rooftop, soon you will be flying,
Down the chimney you will go!
Hurry, Santa, Christmas is a-coming!
Hurry up that ho, ho, ho!

Deck the hall with boughs of holly,
Fa la la la la la la la la.
'Tis the season to be jolly,
Fa la la la la la la.

Hurry, Santa, Christmas is a-coming!
All the world in silence waits.
Hurry, Santa, Christmas is a-coming!
Hurry up, Christmas Day!

Hurry up, Christmas Day!
Christmas is a-coming! Hurry, up!

Perf. 8 Acc. 9

Hurry, Santa!

Words and Music by
David Davenport and
Ruth Elaine Schram

34
soon you will be fly - ing, down the chim - ney you will go!
37
Hur - ry, San - ta, Christ-mas is a - com - ing! Hur-ry up that
40
ho, ho, ho!
2
43-44
Deck the hall with
46
boughs of hol - ly, fa la la la la la la la la.
'Tis the sea - son
50
to be jol - ly, fa la la la la la la.
Hur - ry, San - ta,
54
p
2
Christ-mas is a - com - ing! All the world in si - lence waits.
57-58
59
f
Hur - ry, San - ta, Christ-mas is a - com - ing! Hur-ry up,
62
Christ - mas Day! Hur-ry up, Christ - mas
67
Day! Christ-mas is a - com - ing! Hur-ry up!

The Mountain

Music by Mary Lynn Lightfoot
Words by Emily Dickinson (1830–1886)

The mountain sat upon the plain
In his eternal chair,
His observation omnifold
His inquest ev'rywhere.

The seasons prayed around his knees,
Like children round a sire:
Grandfather of the days is he,
Of dawn the ancestor.

The mountain sat upon the plain
In his eternal chair,
In his eternal chair.

Omnifold: Including everything. (*Omni* means all or everything. As it's used here, *fold* draws on several of its less common meanings, including "to draw together" and "to embrace.")
Inquest: Examination or check up.
Sire: A old word that means both father and ancestor. It can also mean a person of authority.

Emily Dickinson

Now considered one of the greatest American poets in history, Emily Dickinson was nearly unknown in her lifetime. She was an intelligent girl who enjoyed singing and art. An avid reader, Emily often studied the poems of Elizabeth Barrett Browning and Henry David Thoreau. She lived a private life in her family's home in Amherst, Massachusetts, and spent much of her time writing poetry.

Emily wrote over 1,700 poems as well as numerous letters written to her friends and family. Using capitalization, numerous dashes, and common rhyming patterns, Emily created a very unique writing style. A writing critic once tried to change several of her poems into a more traditional format, but Emily refused. She is considered a pioneer in modern poetry for her style and powerful language.

Poetry was a way for Emily to express her feelings towards all aspects of life—love, religion, social status, family, and even death. Many close friends and relatives passed away during Emily's life, and her sadness is often reflected in her poems. It wasn't until after her death, in 1886, that Emily's sister Vinnie found a box of poems and had them published. To think, poems that could have been lost forever are instead some of the most popular pieces of American literature to date.

The Mountain

Perf. 10 Acc. 11

Words by Emily Dickinson (1830–1886)

Music by Mary Lynn Lightfoot

18
I
prayed a - round his knees, like chil - dren round a sire:
II
prayed a - round his knees, like chil - dren round a sire:
22
I
Grand - fa - ther of the days is he, of dawn the an - ces -
II
Grand - fa - ther of the days is he, of dawn the an - ces -
25
I
tor. The moun - tain sat up - on the
II
tor. The moun - tain sat up - on the
29
I
plain in his e - ter - nal chair,
II
plain in his e - ter - nal chair,
32
rit.
a tempo
rit.
I
in his e - ter - nal chair.
rit.
a tempo
rit.
II
in his e - ter - nal chair.

Some Love Coffee

Words and Music by Loretta Mitchell

Orff arrangement by Donna Dirksing

Suggested Grades K–2

Target Concepts

Level bordun
Quarter Notes

Instruments

Triangle with beater
Woodblock
Soprano Glockenspiel (SG)
Soprano (SM) and Alto (AM) Metallophones
Alto (AX) and Bass (BX) Xylophones

Perf. 12 **Acc.** 13

This song is a great way to start music class, and the Orff arrangement can be easily simplified by omitting one or more of the instrument parts.

Process

- Students listen as the teacher sings the first part of the song. Students join in measure 5, echoing the last phrase, "I love children who sing with me."
- Students listen again, joining in on the rest of the song as they become comfortable. The teacher plays the triangle part as the students sing. Eventually, this part is assigned to a student.
- Students pat the AX/BX part while singing. Transfer the pats to the instrumentarium and continue to play throughout the lesson.
- Students clap the SM/AM part while singing. To help reinforce the sustained nature of the part, students should release their hands upward and continue to move them along a circular path until they clap again. Transfer the claps to the instrumentarium.
- Students identify the rhyming words in the song (tea, me; chime, time). Sing the song again. This time, students snap on the rhyming words. Transfer the snaps to the SG.
- Sing the song while playing all instrument parts.

CD Information

The accompaniment recording on Track 13 has a two-bar introduction before the song is played four times (or twice, if you are singing both verses). A four-measure interlude follows and then the song is repeated four times. It ends with a two-bar tag.

Expand It!

- You may use this song to assess students' ability to sing in tune by having a soloist sing the last phrase alone.

Some Love Coffee

Loretta Mitchell
Orff arrangement by Donna Dirksing

Christmas Train

Words and Music by Loretta Mitchell

Orff arrangement by Donna Dirksing

Suggested Grades K–2

Target Concepts

Level bordun
Eighth notes
Form: *D.C. al Fine/Fine* (vocabulary)

Instruments

Cabasa
Train Whistle
Soprano (SX), Alto (AX) and Bass (BX) Xylophones

Perf. 14 **Acc.** 15

Process

- Students sing the song while the teacher plays the cabasa. Repeat the song, with a student playing the cabasa.
- The rest of the class pats the BX ostinato while singing. A few students transfer this part to the BX and play and sing.
- Students speak the "chug-a" rhythm of the SX/AX part while stepping the eighths and moving around the room. Students then sing the song, stepping the eighths during measures 1–4 and standing still for the question and solo answer. (At tempo, this will be close to a run. Remind students that running in the music room is different than running on the playground.) Transfer the SX/AX part to the instrumentarium and sing the song.
- A few students play "choo-choo" on a train whistle on the words "Christ(-mas) train."

CD Information

The accompaniment recording on Track 15 has a four-bar introduction. The song is played six times before the *D.S. al Fine* is taken as written.

Expand It!

Create a Christmas train while preparing the SX/AX part (or as an alternative that simplifies the instrument parts).

- Follow the process above. After students can securely step the eighths of the SX/AX part, have all students not playing the BX part form a train.
- The train "runs" during the first section and stands during the solos. The front student—the engine—plays the train whistle and sings the solo. The student at the end of the line—the caboose—plays the cabasa.
- After singing his or her solo, the engine goes to the end of line, becoming the caboose, and the song is repeated. Repeat until each student has a turn being the engine, or have students form several trains.

Christmas Train

Loretta Mitchell
Orff arrangement by Donna Dirksing

We Wish You a Merry Christmas

Old English

Lesson plan by Patricia Bourne

Orff Arrangement by Linda Forrest

Suggested Grades

Song only: K–3
Instrumentation: 3–6

Target Concepts

Form: ABA, Phrase, *D.S. al fine* (vocabulary)
Meter: $\frac{3}{4}$, pick-up note
Style: Old English carol

Materials

"Which fits?" Reproducible (Mixed Media CD)
ABA visual (Mixed Media CD)

Instruments

Soprano (SX), Alto (AX) and Bass (BX) Xylophones
Soprano Glockenspiel (SG)
Soprano (SM) and
Alto (AM) Metallophones

16 As written (2-bar intro)

17 Accompaniment ♩ = 90 (2-bar intro)

18 Accompaniment ♩ = 98 (2-bar intro)

Although the composer of *We Wish You a Merry Christmas* remains a mystery, its inclusion as a celebrated holiday carol is recognized worldwide. Linda Forrest's arrangement for voices and Orff instruments is pitched well for the youngest of singers, with instrument parts that are challenging for the older elementary student. Perfect for a sing-along or holiday gathering.

Process

- The teacher describes the old British tradition of Christmas carolers going door to door among the wealthy house-owners in attempts to receive food as payment for their singing. The song *We Wish You a Merry Christmas* was among those sung as far back as the 16th century.
- The teacher sings the opening section, asking the younger students to identify which words they hear repeated three times. The older students are asked to identify which rhythm of the three shown below best "fits" the repeated words ("We wish you a merry Christmas").

A larger visual of these rhythms is provided on the mixed-media CD.

- Students join the teacher in singing the A section while tapping the steady beat on the heel of their hands, accentuating the word "wish."
- Older students conclude that the rhythms are grouped in threes and add the correct barlines to the correct rhythmic example (from the "Which fits?" visual). Among your 3–6 graders, a discus-

sion of $\frac{3}{4}$ time could ensue at this time, as could a discussion of the purpose and positioning of the pick-up note.

- Younger students will note the difference between the opening section and the following section by indicating how the words, rhythm and melody differ. Younger students might wish to dramatize the caroling aspect of the song, especially to understand the words "good tidings to you."
- Older students will note a return to the opening section after the middle one, thus recognizing the selection as ABA. A visual you may use to enhance this understanding is provided on the mixed media CD and shown to the right. Younger students would profit from seeing the visuals as well.
- Once the song is learned, the instrument parts may be introduced to older students. (Reproducible Orff parts are included on the mixed-media CD.)

We Wish You a Merry Christmas

Old English
Arranged by Linda Forrest

We wish you a merry Christmas,
We wish you a merry Christmas,
We wish you a merry Christmas,
And a happy New Year!

Good tidings to you,
Wherever you are;
Good tidings for Christmas
And a happy New Year!

We wish you a merry Christmas,
We wish you a merry Christmas,
We wish you a merry Christmas,
And a happy New Year!

We Wish You a Merry Christmas

Old English
Arranged by Linda Forrest

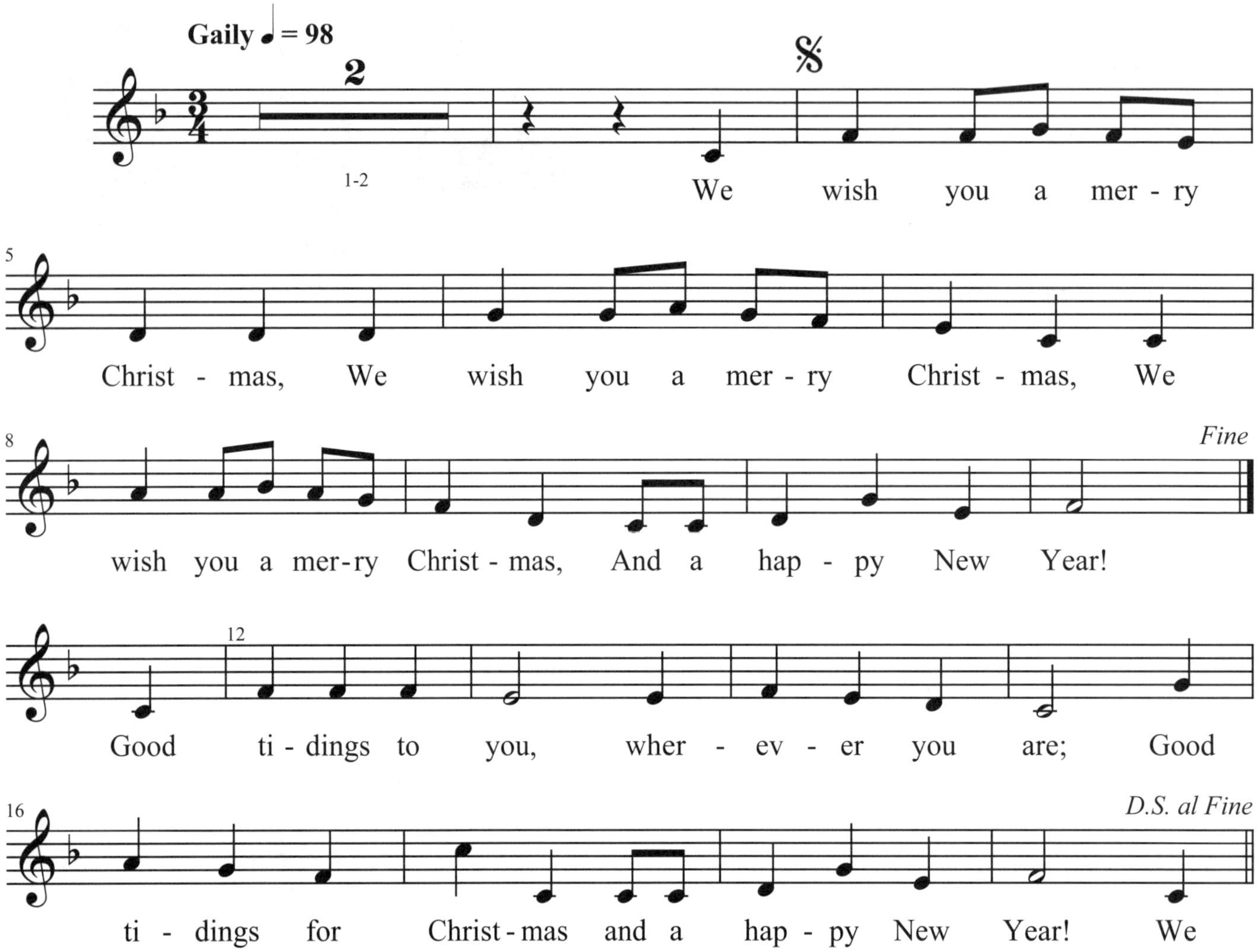

We Wish You a Merry Christmas

16-18

Old English
Arranged by Linda Forrest

10
Fine
hap - py New Year! Good ti - dings to you, wher - ev - er you
SX
AX
SG
SM
AM
BX
15
D.S. al Fine
are; Good ti - dings for Christ - mas and a hap - py New Year! We
SX
AX
SG
SM
AM
BX

IT'S KWANZAA, LET'S CELEBRATE

Lesson plan by Patricia Bourne

Words and Music by Linda Forrest

Suggested Grades 3–6

Target Concepts

Rhythm: Syncopation, tied and dotted notes
Pitch: Harmony, ascending/descending/ repeating tones

Materials

Flashcards (Mixed Media CD)
Xylophone template (Mixed Media CD)

Instruments

Soprano (SG) and Alto (AG) Glockenspiels
Alto (AX) and Bass (BX) Xylophone
Contrabass Bars (CBB)
Claves
Congas

19 As written ♩ = 70

20 As written ♩ = 80

21 Accompaniment

This energetic and appealing composition by veteran music educator Linda Forrest has multiple possibilities for student participation and increased skills. Its syncopated rhythms, harmonically constructed voices, clarity of form, and stylistic appeal make it a sure winner with upper-grade elementary students.

The lesson that follows is a suggested sequence for introducing the syncopated and harmonic patterns of the voices and xylophone parts. Benchmarks are noted to indicate what the students should be able to do before moving to the next steps. Ideas of extended experiences are listed in the "What's Next" section of the lesson. Enjoy *It's Kwanzaa, Let's Celebrate.*

Sequence

- Students step steady beat in place, matching teacher's model, at quarter note = 120.
- When the stepping is together and solid, add a clap on beat 1. Teacher models; students join in, maintaining the steady beat in their feet, as shown in A below.

A.

- Teacher monitors and gradually models more claps. First on 1 and 4 (pattern B below), then gradually the full pattern (C).

B.

C.

- Students transfer the rhythm of their hands to speaking the words "It's Kwanzaa, it's Kwanzaa," stepping the steady beat as they speak.

D.

- Teacher introduces the term *syncopation* to relate to the rhythmic feel experienced by the students

Benchmark 1: Students demonstrate the ability to step the steady beat while clapping and/or speaking a syncopated rhythm.

- Teacher performs/claps pattern E, asking the students to describe how it differs from pattern C.

E. 

- The students join the teacher in pattern F, stepping the beat and speaking the syncopated pattern, "It's Kwanzaa, let's celebrate."

F. 

- Once students are able, they maintain pattern D or F while the teacher chants the other, building student independence while hearing the contrasting rhythms of the xylophone part vs. the vocal part.

Benchmark 2: Students maintain rhythmic independence while hearing a contrasting part.

- The students see each rhythm pattern and discern which chant pattern matches which rhythm. Visuals are provided on the mixed-media CD; Flashcards 1 and 2, respectively. (The topic of tied notes could be addressed at this time, or reserved for later.)
- The teacher shows Flashcard 3, asking how it compares and contrasts to the rhythm visuals (particularly 2). Students should be able to describe subtle differences.
- The students describe how the top note of each chord repeats the pitch while the bottom note steps up, steps down, or remains the same.
- The students sing the top note (G), transferring the words "It's Kwanzaa, let's celebrate." The teacher may sing the contrasting (lower) part while students remain on the G. Switch parts.

Benchmark 3: Students interpret, describe, read, and sing chordal harmony, following the notation pattern as they sing.

- The teacher shows a visual of the alto xylophone part (Flashcard 4). Students may use the xylophone template, provided on the mixed media CD, to practice the part. A review of the rhythm "It's Kwanzaa, it's Kwanzaa" may help solidify the part.
- As students show accuracy on the template, the teacher may place students on xylophones.
- Two parts of the score are ready for combining—the chordal singing and the prominent alto xylophone part.

What's Next

During subsequent lessons, the teacher may want to pursue any or all of the following:

- Add the countermelody (teaching aurally and/or visually).
- Show and add the BX and CBB part (note that the rhythm is a familiar one to students).
- Follow the beat/rhythm sequence when teaching the glockenspiel, conga and clave parts.
- Distinguish and discuss how $\frac{3}{2}$ meter can be interpreted.
- Analyze the form of the piece (ABA).
- Combine multiple classes to perform the entire score.

IT'S KWANZAA, LET'S CELEBRATE

Words and Music by Linda Forrest

Part II
It's Kwanzaa, let's celebrate!
It's Kwanzaa, let's celebrate!
It's Kwanzaa, let's celebrate!
It's Kwanzaa, let's celebrate!

REFRAIN

Part I
Celebrate Kwanzaa!
We join in harmony.
Celebrate Kwanzaa!
We sing in unity.

Part II
It's Kwanzaa, let's celebrate!
It's Kwanzaa, let's celebrate!
It's Kwanzaa, let's celebrate!
It's Kwanzaa, let's celebrate!

Repeat Refrain

Part II
It's Kwanzaa, let's celebrate!
It's Kwanzaa, let's celebrate!

SPOKEN

Part I
Those past and present we commemorate.
"Kuumba,"
"Ujima,"
"Imani,"
"Umoja,"
"Nia,"
"Ujama."

Part II (answers Part I)
These symbols we share and celebrate!
Creativity,
Responsibility,
Faith,
Unity,
Purpose,
Peace.

Sing Refrain twice

Part II
It's Kwanzaa, let's celebrate!
It's Kwanzaa, let's celebrate!
It's Kwanzaa, let's celebrate!
It's Kwanzaa, let's celebrate!

Pronunciation Guide

Kuumba	*koo-OOM-bah*
Ujima	*oo-JEE-mah*
Imani	*ee-MAH-nee*
Umoja	*oo-MOE-jah*
Nia	*nee-AH*
Ujama	*Oo-JAH-mah*

IT'S KWANZAA, LET'S CELEBRATE

Linda Forrest

I
II
Those past and present we com-
Kwan - zaa, let's cel - e - brate!
mem - o - rate.
"Ku-
These sym-bols we share and cel - e - brate!
um-ba,"
"U - ji - ma,"
"I-
Cre-a - tiv - i - ty,
Re-spon-si - bil - i - ty,
man - i,"
"U - mo - ja,"
Faith,
U - ni - ty,
"Ni - a,"
"U - ja - ma."
div.
Pur - pose,
Peace. It's

I
II
Cel - e - brate Kwan - zaa! We join in
Kwan - zaa, let's cel - e - brate! It's Kwan - zaa, let's
har - mo - ny. Cel - e - brate Kwan - zaa!
cel - e - brate! It's Kwan - zaa, let's cel - e - brate! It's
We sing in u - ni - ty.
Kwan - zaa, let's cel - e - brate! It's Kwan - zaa, let's
cel - e - brate! It's Kwan - zaa, let's cel - e - brate! It's
Kwan - zaa, let's cel - e - brate! It's Kwan - zaa, let's cel - e - brate!

IT'S KWANZAA, LET'S CELEBRATE

Linda Forrest

(19) As written 𝅗𝅥 = 70 (20) As written 𝅗𝅥 = 80 (21) Accompaniment

9
I
II
Kwan - zaa, let's cel - e - brate! It's Kwan - zaa, let's cel - e - brate! It's
SG
AG
AX
BX
CBB

13
I
Cel - e - brate Kwan - zaa! We join in har - mo - ny.
II
Kwan - zaa, let's cel - e - brate! It's Kwan - zaa, let's cel - e - brate! It's
SG
AG
AX
BX
CBB

17
I
Cel - e - brate Kwan - zaa! We sing in u - ni - ty.
II
Kwan - zaa, let's cel - e - brate! It's Kwan - zaa, let's cel - e - brate! It's
SG
AG
AX
BX
CBB
21
I
Those
II
Kwan - zaa, let's cel - e - brate! It's Kwan - zaa, let's cel - e - brate!
SG
AG
AX
BX
CBB

25
I
past and pres - ent we com - mem - o - rate.
"Ku-
II
These sym - bols we share and cel - e - brate!
SG
AG
AX
BX
CBB
29
um - ba,"
"U - ji - ma,"
"I -
Cre - a - tiv - i - ty,
Re - spon - si - bil - i - ty,

33
I
II
SG
AG
AX
BX
CBB
man - i,"
"U - mo - ja,"
Faith,
U - ni - ty,

37
I
II
SG
AG
AX
BX
CBB
"Ni - a,"
"U - ja - ma."
div.
Pur - pose,
Peace.
It's

41
I
II
SG
AG
AX
BX
CBB
Cel - e - brate Kwan - zaa! We join in har - mo - ny.
Kwan - zaa, let's cel - e - brate! It's Kwan - zaa, let's cel - e - brate! It's
45
Cel - e - brate Kwan - zaa! We sing in u - ni - ty.
Kwan - zaa, let's cel - e - brate! It's Kwan - zaa, let's cel - e - brate! It's

49
I
II
Kwan - zaa, let's cel - e - brate! It's Kwan - zaa, let's cel - e - brate! It's
SG
AG
AX
BX
CBB
53
I
II
Kwan - zaa, let's cel - e - brate! It's Kwan - zaa, let's cel - e - brate!
SG
AG
AX
BX
CBB

We Got the Beat

by Mark Burrows

Suggested Grades 3–6

22-30

The percussive possibilities of the human voice make it a great addition to the instrumentarium, and one that is convenient, adaptable and inexpensive. In the three activities that follow, students will have the opportunity to explore timbres, strengthen their rhythmic and steady beat skills, and work with a classic poem.

Alpha-Beat Soup

The alphabet is rich with wonderful, colorful percussive sounds, with each letter possessing its own character, from the explosive "B" to the warm "V." Much of that character comes from how the sound is formed, which is also the primary way consonants are categorized. Voiced consonants are those which use the vocal chords, and so contain pitch. Unvoiced consonants use the articulators (lips, teeth, tongue) without the aid of the voice, and so do not contain pitch. Below are some of the English language consonants. Where possible, the unvoiced consonant is shown next to its voiced cousin.

Voiced Consonant	*Unvoiced Consonant*
B	P
D	T
G	K
J	CH
L	
M	
N	
R	
V	F
Z	S
ZH	SH

Lead-up Activity

Begin by inviting students to experiment with different consonants and consonant combinations, mixing and matching to find cool, new sounds. Some suggestions you may offer:

- Try using different pitches to affect the sound of the voiced consonants.
- Try different mouth positions to give each consonant a different resonance. For example, an "uh" vowel formation will make a vocalized "D" sound deeper and richer. An "ih" vowel formation will make a vocalized "D" sound brighter.
- Experiment with consonant sounds from non-English languages, including the rolled "R" (Italian, Spanish), the guttural "CH" (German), and the glottal, which is produced by the quick release of built-up air behind the vocal folds (Chinese dialect of *Tsou*).

Rhythm Patterns

The two rhythm patterns that follow utilize the sounds of different consonants. The first uses three different voiced consonants while the other highlights three unvoiced consonants. Use the layering process, as suggested below, to expand either one into a 16-measure piece. (The Voiced and Unvoiced rhythms are performed in this manner on Tracks 22 and 23, respectively.)

Suggested Form

- Part 1 enters and performs for 4 measures.
- Part 2 joins and they perform together for 4 measures.
- Part 3 joins and all perform for 8 measures
- End with a strong cutoff after beat 4 or have all students make their sound on a strong downbeat.

The two rhythms may also be combined into one piece—students chant the voiced rhythm for several measures; switch to the unvoiced rhythm for several more measures; then return to the voiced rhythm and finish the piece. In this scenario, all parts may enter together or you could use the layering process to build each section, then groove for a few measures once all parts are in, then signal the next pattern and begin building it.

Other options include:

- Using these rhythms as accompaniments for rhymes, chants or songs.
- Adding other alphabet sounds to create a stand-alone percussion piece. These parts could be written by students in small groups, or you could invite soloists to improvise over the groove.
- Changing dynamics and/or tempo to further add variety. You could conduct gradual or immediate changes, or invite a student to conduct the group.

Alpha-Beat Soup

22 Voiced

Part 1

Part 2

Part 3

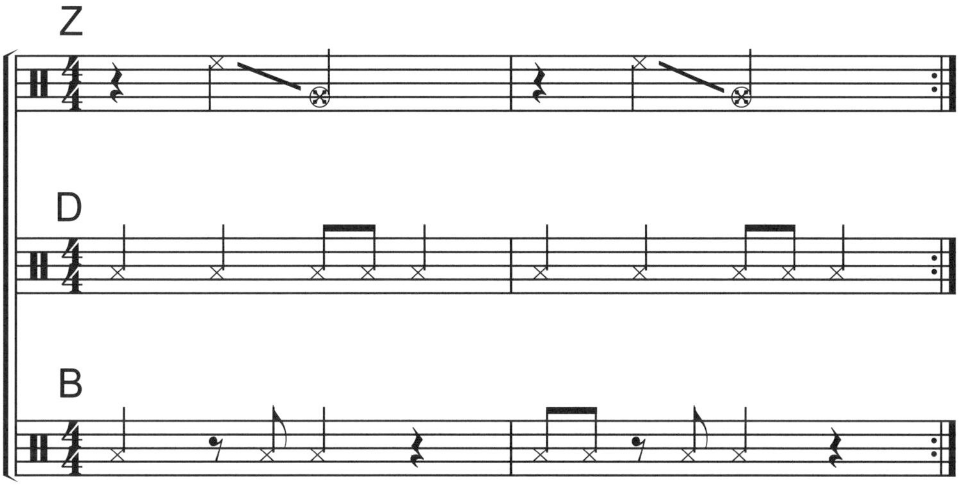

23 Unvoiced

Part 1

Part 2

Part 3

Beatboxing

Over the past few decades hip-hop has emerged as a powerful force in the world of popular music. As hip-hop has developed, so has the art of vocal percussion known as *beatboxing.* Beatboxing often uses consonants and consonant clusters to imitate the sounds of drums, cymbals, and even scratch records.

The following are some common beatboxing sounds and the instruments they imitate. They are announced and modeled on Track 24.

24

Beatboxing Sound	*Instrument*
Psh	big crash cymbal
Ksh	small crash cymbal
Ts	high hat
D(uh)	bass drum
G(uh)	bass drum (electronic)
Kh	snare
Chk	techno-snare
D(ih)-g(ah) d(ih)-g(ah) [high to low]	toms
Wh(ih)k(uh)-wh(ih)k(uh)-wh(ih)k	scratch record
Bm or Dm	low drum
Pfpfpf	techno-drum
Glottal*	techno bass drum

**This glottal is performed with the tongue against the teeth at the roof of the mouth.*

These beatboxing sounds are traditionally performed by one person while another chants or raps a text. Okay, I said it. Rap...they rap the text. Mention the words "rap" or "hip-hop" and you're bound to elicit a strong response. Detractors will point to the occasional negative messages presented in the text. Supporters will point out the rhythmic vitality and cultural relevance of rap and hip-hop. If the text seems to be the major stumbling block, choose your own text, such as a famous poem or nursery rhyme. You could even have students rap the times tables.

Begin by inviting students to experiment with these sounds, first by just making them, then by combining a few, in time, to create a pattern. A few examples are provided on the facing page, and they are modeled on Tracks 25–28 on the *Activate!* CD.

From here, the class could perform the Group Beatbox provided on the next page, and modeled on Track 29, or students could work in small groups to create their own beatbox. Once a groove is established, you could invite a student to rap over it. Students could rap about something they're learning in school, in music or another subject, their family, their favorite sports team or band—the possibilities are nearly endless.

Beatbox Solos

Mark Burrows

25 **Techno-beat**

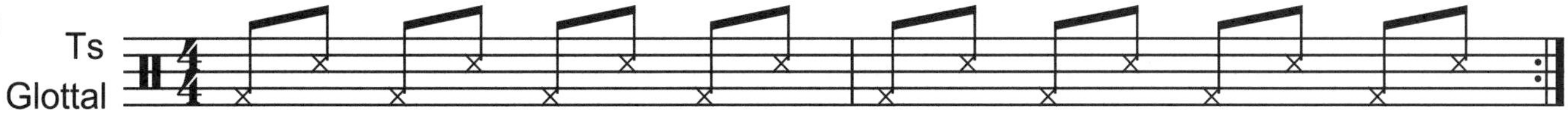

26 **Rock**

27 **Rock II**

28 **Waltz**

Group Beatbox

Mark Burrows

29 **Intro:**

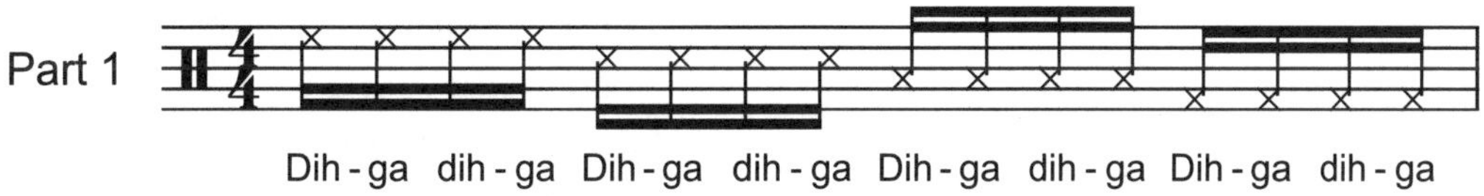

Groove:

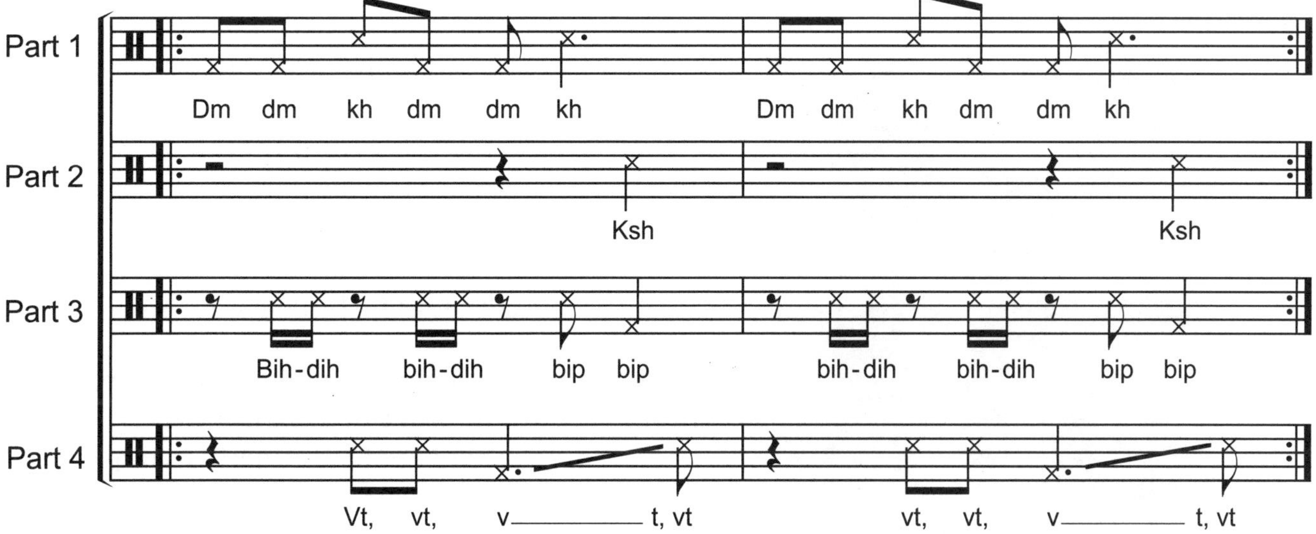

How Doth the Little Crocodile Poetry Slam

In case you haven't frequented a coffee shop or college bar lately, poetry slams are competitive events where people perform their (usually) original poems in a stylized manner that borrows a lot from hip-hop. Some accompany this spoken word art with beatboxing, which is what we're going to do here.

Process

Divide the students into two groups. One group performs the beatbox while the other group chants *How Doth the Little Crocodile,* by Lewis Carroll, in rhythm. Then, have the groups switch parts.

Try the following extension, particularly with your older students:

1. Divide the students into pairs. Hand each pair an index card with a short, classic poem. (A few examples are provided on the right, or, in the true spirit of a poetry slam, you could invite students to use a poem they've written, perhaps in their Language Arts class.)
2. Have the students in each pair find the rhythm inherent in the poem and compose a beatbox to accompany a rhythmic reading of the poem.
3. Have the pairs rap/beatbox their poems for the others.
4. Afterwards, combine the rapper of one poem with the beatboxer of another. Does the beatbox seem to complement the poem or distract from it?

Hope

"Hope" is the thing with feathers –
That perches in the soul –
And sings the tune without the words –
And never stops – at all –

And sweetest – in the Gale – is heard –
And sore must be the storm –
That could abash the little Bird
That kept so many warm –

I've heard it in the chillest land –
And on the strangest sea –
Yet, never, in Extremity,
It asked a crumb – of Me.

—Emily Dickinson (1830–1886)

The Eagle

He clasps the crag with crooked hands;
Close to the sun in lonely lands,
Ringed with the azure world, he stands.

The wrinkled sea beneath him crawls;
He watches from his mountain walls,
And like a thunderbolt he falls.

—Alfred, Lord Tennyson (1809–1892)

There Was a Young Lady Whose Nose

There was a young lady whose Nose
Continually prospers and grows;
When it grew out of sight,
She exclaimed in a fright,
"Oh! Farewell to the end of my Nose!"

—Edward Lear (1812–1888)

Hurt No Living Thing

Hurt no living thing:
Ladybird, no butterfly,
Nor moth with dusty wing,
No cricket chirping cheerily,

Nor grasshopper so light of leap,
Nor dancing gnat, no beetle fat,
Nor harmless worms that creep.

—Christina Rossetti (1830–1894)

How Doth the Little Crocodile

Poetry Slam

30

Words by Lewis Carroll (1832–1898)
Music by Mark Burrows

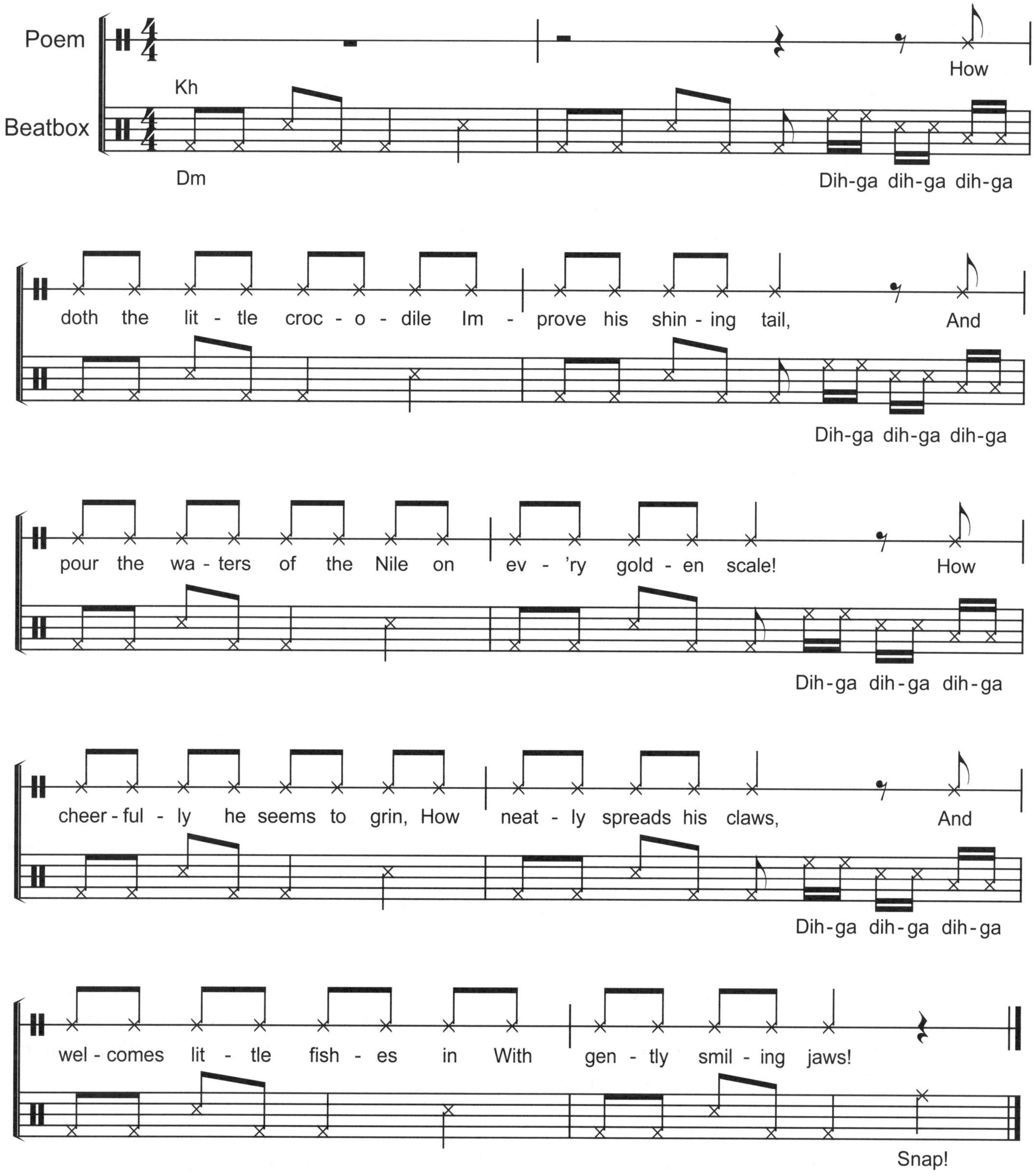

Exploring Melody Through Movement

by Beth Bryant

There are many ways to define the musical concept of *melody.* "Melody is a pathway of notes" is the definition that I use with students. This way of thinking about melody works well when students are also receiving a conceptually based physical education program that encourages them to link movement with language and thought. This article describes how you can assist students in developing an understanding of the abstract concept of melody by helping them represent melodic elements with movement.

One way to begin this process is to encourage students to use nonlocomotor movements (anchored movements, such as moving the arms or legs while seated) to represent a melodic pathway. For example, have students represent a pathway with their hands and then try to sing a melody that goes with it. Alternately, a student could sing first, and the other students could try to make the pathway that they have just heard. (For instance, if a student sings a melody that goes up, then down, then up again, the students would follow that pathway with their hands.)

In these early explorations, we recommend starting with nonlocomotor movements because translating the abstract concept of melody into movement may not come easily at first. Nonlocomotor movements are easier to coordinate with music than locomotor movements (movements with weight transfers, such as stepping in place, walking, or skipping). Another strategy to remember in conducting these activities is that melodies should be sung without words: the teacher or student should sing the melody on a neutral syllable, such as "Bah," or hum it. At this point words would distract students from the lesson's focus on melodic elements.

Another way to make melody more concrete for children is to show them a vertical keyboard (a set of bells or a xylophone turned on end), with the lower notes closest to the floor. With the keyboard positioned in this way, they can visualize melodies going up, down, staying the same, or moving by steps or skips.

When students have had little experience with the concept of melody, their initial exploration of melodies should focus on just two possibilities for how melodies can move. For example, when working in grades K–2, or with beginners of any age, have students compare melodies that go up with melodies that stay on the same pitch, using nonlocomotor movement to represent this. For example, for melodies that go up, their hands would move upward, and for melodies that stay the same, their hands would stay in the same place or track from left to right on the same plane. A variation is to have students use their whole bodies to represent the melody, for example, going from squatting to standing for melodies that go up. Another lesson might compare melodies that go down with melodies that stay the same.

While these activities may seem too easy, students who are not used to listening to melodies initially have a very difficult time aurally identifying melodies that stay the same. With older and/or more experienced students, you can revisit these lessons later using locomotor movement. In this case, students might represent melodies that stay on the same pitch by stepping in place and melodies that go up or down by traveling forward or backward in a circle (or toward or away from one wall of the classroom). Once students have had experience representing and interpreting movements that stand for two possibilities, they are ready to work with all three at once.

Another subconcept of melody to present to students is the difference between a step (moving from one note to the next as in a scale) and a skip (moving from one note to the next, passing over one or more notes). Demonstrating steps and skips on a set of bells, a xylophone, or a metallophone is helpful because students can actually *see* the difference. Students can continue to explore this difference through movement, for example, traveling using small, close-together steps (steps) or further-apart steps (skips). Note that when working with *step* versus *skip* it is also important to differentiate the movement of skipping from the musical term *skip.*

Students can explore these concepts further by working in pairs, with one partner traveling and the other representing the partner's pathway by playing a classroom keyboard instrument. One student would play a melody that goes by step, and the partner would walk on a pathway of paper plates, carpet squares, or floor tiles, stepping on each object in order. If the student player plays a melody of skips, then the traveler would step on every other object, or every third object. The order of this activity can and should be reversed, with the first partner traveling and the second partner playing a melody that matches. With either of these activities, it is easiest if the pathway is all steps or all skips. When children are ready for the challenge, you can give them the option of combining steps and skips in their pathway or melody.

All of the activities presented here should initially be carried out with random melodies that are not attached to any song. In beginning experiences, students could "sing" as if using a slide whistle, doing a *glissando* (a slurring of pitches in which there is one long sound going up or down rather than separate notes) to represent melodies going up or down. To represent skips, students would sing distinct notes in contrasting pitches (using very high or very low notes).

Teachers sometimes don't understand the importance of introducing melodic concepts by working first with random pitches rather than with specific songs. Yet this simplified approach usually results in a better understanding of the underlying concepts of melody than the traditional approach. Students who have this foundation will be much more successful later on when trying to decode, sight-sing, or notate melodies. Keep in mind also that steady beat and rhythm are not used

in these experiences. When working with the concept of melody, especially with beginners, there should be no timing involved at first. After students have a good foundation and really understand melody and its subconcepts, they will be ready to combine the many concepts involved when singing or playing a song.

Beginning on the next page are two related activities, one suitable for grades K–2, the other for grades 3–6. Both of these activities will be more successful if students have already had a chance to explore elements of melody in some of the experiences suggested above. Since all these experiences and activities allow students to choose what to do and decide how to represent what they know, we as teachers can immediately assess their level of understanding and determine where to focus our attention in future lesson plans. [!]

Melody Pathways

Grades K–2

Concepts/Objectives

- Melody
- Melodic direction
- Moving to music
- Moving up and down

Materials

Recorder, set of step bells, or xylophone
Yarn, markers or paint, and white paper or whiteboard (optional, for extension)

Music

Melodies

Summary

Students must understand what a melody is before they can describe melodies that they already know "by heart." In this activity, students explore melodic directions and learn *Melodies*, found on page 61, in preparation for future work with the concept of melody.

Procedure

1. Ask your students, "What is melody?" Solicit and accept as many different answers as possible. If the students have little or no background or reference point for answering such a broad question, you could try a comparative question such as "What is the difference between melody and steady beat?" or "What is the difference between melody and rhythm?" You could also sing the initial question, using a very familiar or very unusual melody to elicit students' answers.
2. Sing a *glissando* (a slurring of notes going upward or downward), and ask students to show with their hands or whole bodies in which direction the glissando is moving. Sing a single, sustained pitch, and ask students to show with their hands or whole bodies what they hear.
3. Ask students what they noticed as they moved.
4. Have one student come to the front of the group and move his or her hands upward or downward. See if the class can copy the movement and add vocal sounds that correctly follow the direction of the movement. (For instance, if the student moves his/her hands upward, the class would move their hands upward and also make an upward glissando with their voices.) Continue with other students moving their hands or their whole bodies going up or down or staying the same.

5. Ask students which step was easier or harder—listening to a melody and using movement to show what they heard or watching and copying a leader's movements and then making the melody with their voices. (This step allows you to assess students' understanding to this point.)
6. On a recorder, a set of bells or a xylophone, play the first phrase of *Melodies* (C-D-E-F-G or do-re-mi-fa-so in any key of your choice), and ask students to show what they hear with their hands or their whole bodies. Repeat this process with each of the remaining three phrases. The last phrase may be a challenge for them; at this point, it is fine if students mention only that the melody goes up and down and do not make a distinction between steps versus skips.
7. Speak the words of the song (without any melody) phrase by phrase, and ask the students to move their hands in the appropriate direction and try to make a melody with their voices that would go with the words.
8. Sing the first phrase ("Melodies step up") several times. Have the students join in when they are ready and move in the appropriate direction. Repeat for each phrase. (It is important that you only sing and do not demonstrate movements for students to copy. By taking care not to move, you ensure that the students have to process the words to the song as they generate their own matching movements.)
9. Combine two of the phrases, and see if the students can sing and move to the two phrases together. Sing the whole song, and have students move to the whole song as they listen to it. Those students who are ready can sing as they move.

Facilitation and Reflection

- What have you learned about melody?
- What songs do you know that have melodies that go up? Go down? Stay the same?
- What do we call things that have steady beat or rhythm but do not use melody? (Rhymes, chants, poems)

Extensions

- If you have a typical greeting that you sing with your classes, try altering the melody of the greeting each day. Have students join in singing the melody, use movement to show its direction, and then identify the direction.
- Students can sing the greeting using one of the melodic phrases from *Melodies*, or they can sing their own created melody for a greeting or a closing to a class.
- Students can try to "notate" or represent melodic direction using yarn or lines drawn or painted on paper or whiteboards.

Melodies

Elizabeth Carlton

Melody Detectives

Grades 3–6

Concepts/Objectives

- Melody
- Melodic direction
- Step versus skip
- Moving to music

Materials

One or more sets of step bells
Xylophone (optional, for extension)

Music

Melodies; Hot Cross Buns; Mary Had a Little Lamb; and *Twinkle, Twinkle, Little Star*

Summary

Once students have a basic understanding of the concept of melody, they can begin exploring and playing the actual melodies from songs that they know by heart. Starting from a movement foundation and then extending this by using classroom instruments, students can become successful "melody detectives."

Procedure

1. Ask students what they know about the concept of melody. Solicit and accept many answers. Sing *Melodies*, found on page 61, and ask students to show the melody with movement as they sing.
2. Repeat the singing of the song, showing the melody phrase by phrase and questioning students as follows. After "Melodies step up" ask, "How many notes were there?" (five) After "Melodies step down" ask, "How many notes?" (five) "Were they the same or different as the notes in the first phrase?" (the same) "Was the direction of the melody the same or different?" (different) After "Melodies can stay the same" ask, "How many notes?" (one) "Was it a new note or one that has already been used?" (one that has already been used—the highest one) After "or skip up and down" ask, "How many notes were there?" (three) "Which ones?" (Depending on how you have been identifying notes with students, they may answer "5, 3, 5, 3, 1" or say something like "High, middle, high, middle, low.") Ask, "How many bells would be needed to play the song?" (five)
3. Arrange a set of step bells in order from lowest to highest, with the first five steps (C-D-E-F-G) in the song. If you have multiple sets of step bells, students could split into small groups to try to figure out how to play the song on the step bells. Otherwise, ask, "Who thinks they could play the melody for the first phrase ("Melodies step up") on the step bells?"
4. Repeat this process with each phrase. If the student volunteer plays correctly, the next student plays the next phrase. If not, the next student must say what mistake needs to be corrected in order to get the next turn to try playing the melody correctly. (If the students have been in small groups, pick one group at a time to play each phrase and ask the other groups if the melody was correct or not.)
5. After the song has been played correctly once through, the students (or small-group volunteers) that play after this can play any phrase from the song that they choose, with the rest of the class echoing and showing what they heard (singing on a neutral syllable, such as "la" or "loo"). Then ask if somebody can identify the phrase that was played to get the next turn. There can be as many turns as time permits.
6. Ask the students to think of examples of very simple songs that they know whose melodies could be represented by hand movements. Sing these songs and have students show the melodic direction. You may have to have some hints ready to facilitate this step. For instance, *Twinkle, Twinkle, Little Star* is a difficult melody to start out with because the melody pathway is mixed (two notes the same, a skip up, another note the same, then a step up, and so on). This kind of pathway is more difficult for children to perceive initially than those that those with fewer changes in the pattern. *Mary Had a Little Lamb* is a bit easier than *Twinkle*, and *Hot Cross Buns* is easier still.

7. Pick one song (*Hot Cross Buns* would be the easiest to start with), and set up students in small groups with the correct number of bells in their group. Challenge students to become "melody detectives" by trying to play *Hot Cross Buns* on their bells. Groups can perform for each other when they are ready. Continue with other songs as students are ready and able.

Facilitation and Reflection

- What other melodies do you think you could figure out?
- What other songs have melodies that only move by skip? By step?
- What songs do you know that use the same melody? (*Alphabet Song; Twinkle, Twinkle, Little Star;* and *Baa, Baa, Black Sheep)*

Extensions

- Students can be melody detectives using a full set of bells or a xylophone (these have more notes than necessary).
- Students can try to decode more complex melodies.

Hot Cross Buns

Mary Had a Little Lamb

Twinkle, Twinkle, Little Star

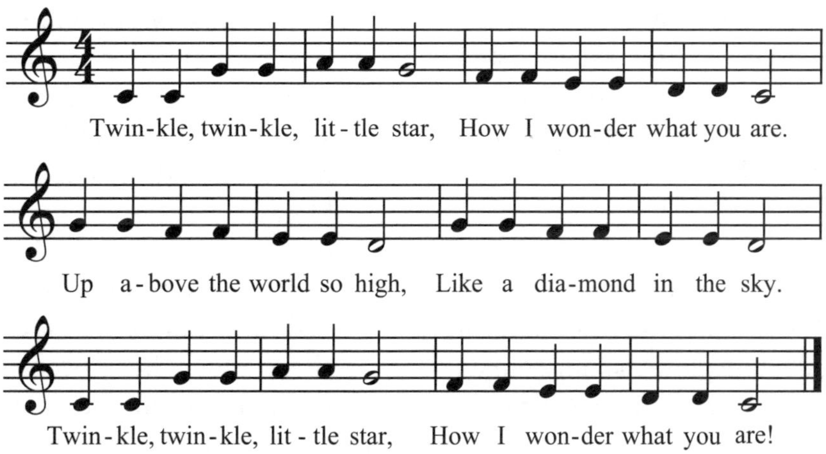

Exploring the Recorder

by Beth Bryant

Grades 3–4

Concepts/Objectives

- Exploring purposeful movement
- Moving to music
- Responding to visual movement directions
- Representing musical patterns with movement

Materials

Recorders (one per student if possible)

Music

Hot Cross Buns

Too often, in performance-based curricular areas such as learning a musical instrument, we resort to drilling on skills rather than setting up experiences that allow students to explore new concepts, apply previously learned information, and demonstrate their understanding. There are many concepts that students can discover, explore, and represent through movement during the initial stages of playing the recorder. This lesson will serve as a guide and a jumping-off point not only for beginning recorder, but also for a movement-oriented and concept-based approach to other beginning instruments.

Summary

In this activity, students explore making different sounds, first using the recorder head joint only and then the whole recorder. They discover ways to make long and short, high and low, and upward and downward sounds, and they play rhythm patterns. Students represent these sound and rhythm patterns with movement.

Procedure

1. Ask students how many different sounds they think they can make with just the head joint of the recorder. Let students explore making sounds with only the head joint. (In a very small room, teachers may want to have only a few students explore at a time while other students represent what they hear with movements, as in Step 2.)
2. Student leaders take turns playing the sounds they have discovered while the rest of the class enacts with movement what they hear the leader playing. For example, if the student leader plays high and low sounds (achieved by playing the head joint open, and then closing the bottom of the head joint with the hand over the end that fits onto the body of the recorder), then the class would show this by putting their hands over their heads for the high sounds and on the floor or their laps for the low sounds. If the leader plays sounds that go up and down (produced by having one finger slide in and out of the head joint while blowing a sustained sound) then the other students would reflect this by moving their hands up and down in front of them. If the leader plays fast and slow sounds, the class can represent this with short and jerky movements or slow, sustained movements with their hands or feet.

3. Students can also be conductors, performing movements with their hands as in Step 2 while the rest of the class plays on their head joints what they see being conducted.
4. With the head joint or the entire recorder, students explore playing rhythm patterns from familiar songs. This will help them begin to develop proper articulation (using the tongue to modulate the sound, rather than just blowing). To start this, the leader plays or sings the rhythm of a simple song, such as *Hot Cross Buns* (see page 63), on a single note. The rest of the class then echoes the leader's patterns by playing the rhythm on their recorders, clapping, or stepping. The students then try to guess the song from which the pattern comes.

Facilitation and Reflection

- How many different sounds or concepts could you represent using just the head joint of the recorder?
- Which was easier, to be a playing conductor or a moving conductor? Why?
- Which was easier, to be a playing follower or a moving follower? Why?

Extension

- When listening to leaders play a pattern, have the followers close their eyes and process the sounds aurally before echoing or responding with movement.

Partner Formations in Folk Dance

by Phyllis S. Weikart

Partner formations, especially male/female pairs, are common in folk dance as well as in other forms of dance. This article explains some common formations used in partner and mixer folk dances. First, here are some general teaching strategies to use before asking students to take a partner or join hands with a partner.

General Partner Strategies

1. Begin with mixer dances, in which partners change with each repetition of the dance, and have students do the dances without holding hands. When students are not holding hands, they tend to be less concerned about doing the dance "right" before they've had a chance to practice it sufficiently.
2. Start with dances that don't require a specific correct foot throughout the dance; students will be more successful. Movements around the circle in a forward or backward direction, movements toward and away from the center of the circle, and dance steps in place generally do not require a correct foot. Sideward dance movements and crossover steps require a correct starting foot.
3. Teach the dance as a single-circle dance first, assuming the role one of the partners will have later, when you do the dance in pairs. For example, teach the outside or girl's part without hands held. At this point students do not know the dance is going to be a partner or couple dance. Students are less easily embarrassed when learning a dance without a partner.
4. Have students learn both the inside (male) and outside (female) parts of the dance if the only real change is the starting foot. This strategy assumes the dance is identical for both partners.
5. Think about whether the dance you've selected can be done with any pairing (boy/boy, girl/girl, or boy/girl) or requires boy/girl partners. Many elementary-age students are much more comfortable in the beginning taking a partner of the same sex, so giving them a choice greatly reduces problems initially. When students are comfortable with the dance, you may then suggest they take a partner of the opposite sex.
6. When students first take partners, allow them if possible to simply hold hands or use a double-shoulder hold instead of the shoulder-waist hold. These ways of connecting are more acceptable to students in the beginning. (In the double-shoulder hold, partners face each other and hold each other's shoulders with arms straight. In the shoulder-waist position, male and female partners face each other with the male holding the female's waist and the female holding the male's shoulders. Arms are straightened.)

Basic Formation

Following are some descriptions of three basic partner formations, holds, and positions:

- **Single circle.** Partners stand side by side in a single circle facing toward the center or around the circle clockwise or counterclockwise. *Sellenger's Round*, on page 67, uses this formation.
- **Double circle (partners facing counterclockwise or clockwise), "V" or "W" hold.** Partners are arranged side by side in concentric circles with both dancers facing in the same direction. (*Apat-Apat,* on page 70, uses this formation.) Hands usually are joined in a simple "V" hold (holding hands with the inside person's hand facing forward and supporting the outside person's hand). A "W" hold or a little-finger hold may also be used. (In the "W" and little-finger holds, partners join hands or little fingers at shoulder level with their elbows bent; the inside person's hand faces forward and supports the outside person's hand or fingers.)
- **Skater's hold.** Partners are side by side facing the same direction counterclockwise or clockwise around the double circle. Right hands are joined in front of the right-hand person and left hands are joined in front of the left-hand person. Right hands are on top and left hands underneath. *Mexican Mixer*, on page 72, uses the skater's hold. (!)

Sellenger's Round

(SELL-ing-gur's Round)

Grades 2–6

Music

Sellenger's Round (31)

Sellinger's Round is one of the best known of England's "historical" country dances. In contrast to country dances that were handed down informally, the historical dances had more complex patterns and were documented and published. A version of this dance appeared in 1670 in a collection by John Playford, an English bookseller and musician.

Note: In the dance notation, the words in italics and parentheses are English dance terms. Definitions are provided on page 69.

Lead-up activities and teaching suggestions are provided at the end of the dance directions.

Introduction: 8 macrobeats

Formation: Partners in a single circle

Part IA

Clockwise

SLIDE / &	SLIDE / &	SLIDE / &	SLIDE / &	SLIDE / &	SLIDE / &	SLIDE / &	SLIDE / HOP
L R	L R	L R	L R	L R	L R	L R	L L

Counterclockwise

SLIDE / &	SLIDE / &	SLIDE / &	SLIDE / &	SLIDE / &	SLIDE / &	STEP	STEP
R L	R L	R L	R L	R L	R L	R	L

Beats 1–8 Slide 7 steps sideward clockwise followed by a step L foot sideward left and a hop L foot (*Slipping*).

9–16 Slide 6 steps sideward counterclockwise followed by a step R foot sideward R and a step L foot in place.

Part II

IN / CLOSE	IN	IN / CLOSE	IN	OUT	OUT	OUT	OUT
R L	R	L R	L	R	L	R	L

STEP / STEP	STEP	STEP / STEP	STEP	TURN	TURN	TURN	TURN
R L	**R**	**L R**	**L**	**R**	**L**	**R**	**L**

REPEAT PART II

Beats 1–2 Two-step in, beginning R foot (*Setting*).
3–4 Two-step in, beginning L foot.
5–8 Step R, L, R, L foot out (*Out a double*) and turn to face partner.
9–12 Two balances (*Three-steps*) in place beginning R foot, L foot facing partner (*Setting to partner*), leaping onto the first step of each three-step.
13–16 Full turn R, L, R, L foot clockwise (*Turn single*).
17–32 Repeat Part II, beats 1–16.

Part IB

IN	IN	IN	IN	OUT	OUT	OUT	OUT
R	**L**	**R**	**L**	**R**	**L**	**R**	**L**

REPEAT

Beats 1–4 Step R, L, R, L foot in (*In a double*).
5–8 Step R, L, R, L foot out (*Out a double*).
9–16 Repeat Part IB, beats 1–8.

Part II

Repeat Part II, beats 1–32.

Part IC

FWD	FWD	FWD	PIVOT	FWD	FWD	FWD	PIVOT
R	**L**	**R**	**(R)**	**L**	**R**	**L**	**(L)**

REPEAT

Beats 1–3 Step R, L, R foot changing places with partner; females moving inside clockwise and males outside counterclockwise; keep facing partner (*Siding*).
4 Pivot ½ while continuing to face partner.
5–8 Step L, R, L foot back to place along same path (keep looking at partner).
9–16 Repeat Part IC, beats 1–8.

Part II

Repeat Part II, beats 1–32.

Part ID

TURN (R ELBOW)	TURN	TURN	TURN	TURN	TURN	AWAY	AWAY
R	**L**	**R**	**L**	**R**	**L**	**R**	**L**

REPEAT OPPOSITE DIRECTION (L ELBOW)

Beats 1–8 R elbow turn with partner (*Arming*)—move apart on beats 7–8.
9–16 L elbow turn (move apart on beats 15–16).

Part II

Repeat Part II, beats 1–32.

Part IA

Repeat Part IA, beats 1–16 (*Slipping*).

Part II

Repeat Part II, beats 1–32.

Lead-up Activities: Practice SLIDES (individual tempo). Practice TWO-STEPS (individual tempo). Practice STEP/STEP, STEP in place (individual tempo). Practice TURNS to the right in 4 steps (individual tempo).

Teaching Suggestions: Practice Part II, beats 1–8, with a partner (partner beat then SAY & DO). Add on the BALANCE (in-place THREE-STEP) with partners facing each other and then the full TURN clockwise. SAY & DO Part II. Learn Part IA, B, C, D, repeating Part II after each (SAY & DO). SAY & DO the entire dance and then add the music.

Chair Dancing: Do the verses in place or away from and toward the chair. Substitute steps in place for the TURN in part II.

Definitions

Arming Elbow turn with R and then L elbows.

In a Double Four steps toward the center of the circle.

Out a Double Four steps away from the center of the circle.

SAY & DO A learning strategy in which students label a movement with a single word and speak that label as they do it. For example, students use the words APART and TOGETHER to label the leg movements in a jumping jacks sequence. Once students are secure with the leg pattern, arm movements are added. Students then SAY & DO the leg movements (APART, TOGETHER), integrating them with the arm movements. The integrated movement pattern is repeated until students can do the movement without having to think about it.

Setting Two-step toward the center of the circle (see definition below for two-step).

Setting to partner Setting facing partner.

Siding Walking forward in opposite directions as if on the rails of a train track.

Slipping Sliding sideward around the circle.

Three-step Three steps danced in any direction or in place in a 1& 2 rhythmic pattern where "1&" is a divided beat (e.g., STEP/STEP, STEP).

Turn single A full turn carried out individually by each partner.

Two-step Three steps danced in any direction or in place in a 1& 2 rhythmic pattern where "1&" is a divided beat and a closing step is the second movement (e.g., IN/CLOSE, IN).

Apat-Apat

(AH-paht AH-paht)
Four by Four

Grades 2–6

Music
Apat-Apat (32)

This dance from the Philippines celebrates the planting of rice, a major food in Philippine culture. *Apat-Apat* was first taught to North American folk dancers in 1961 by Francisco Aquino, a physical education instructor at the state university in Manila. A simple mixer dance, *Apat-Apat* has been popular for many years in recreational groups and is enjoyable for elementary students.

Lead-up activities and teaching suggestions are provided at the end of the dance directions.

Introduction: Pickup plus 8 microbeats

Formation: Partners, double circle facing counterclockwise, inside hands joined

Note: Keep steps small and the movements continuous. This should not be a march. No R foot or L foot needs to be specified.

Part I

Counterclockwise / *Clockwise*

FWD	FWD	FWD	TURN (½)	FWD	FWD	FWD	TURN (¼)
R	L	R	L	R	L	R	L

AWAY	AWAY	AWAY	AWAY	TOWARD	TOWARD	TOWARD	TOWARD
R	L	R	L	R	L	R	L

FWD	FWD	FWD	FWD	BWD	BWD	BWD	BWD
R	L	R	L	R	L	R	L

Counterclockwise (beats 5–8)

TURN	TURN	TURN	TURN	FWD (CHANGE)	FWD	FWD	FWD
R	L	R	L	R	L	R	L

Beats 1–4	Step R, L, R, L foot forward counterclockwise (on beat 4 release hands and execute ½ turn right to face clockwise).
5–8	Step R, L, R, L foot forward clockwise; end facing partner.
9–12	Back away from each other—R, L, R, L foot.
13–16	Walk toward each other—R, L, R, L foot, end with ¼ turn right (males face clockwise, females counterclockwise).
17–20	Walk forward 4 steps (inside circle clockwise, outside counterclockwise).
21–24	Walk backward 4 steps to meet partner (turn to face partner).
25–28	Turn with partner 4 steps clockwise (R forearms together).
29–32	Outside person turn ½ turn in 4 steps while inside person walks R, L, R, L foot forward counterclockwise to new partner.

Lead-up Activities: Practice walking 4 steps, turning ¼, then moving in the new direction either FORWARD or BACKWARD until comfortable with directional changes (individual tempo). Practice walking 4 steps, execute a ½ TURN on the fourth step; then WALK 4 steps in the other direction. Practice walking BACKWARD 4 steps, followed by walking FORWARD 4 steps.

Teaching Suggestions: Practice each combination of 8 beats with a partner (partner beat). Practice the transitions after each set of 8 beats. Practice the 4-step TURN with a partner (partner beat). Combine the parts of the dance (SAY & DO).

Mexican Mixer

Grades 2–6

Music

Mexican Mixer 33

Mexican Mixer, originally choreographed by Texas dance teacher Nelda Drury, is based on polka rhythms that were popular in Mexico during the reign of Emperor Maximilian, a member of the Austrian royal family who was installed by Napoleon and ruled from 1864 to 1867. This was a period of renewed European influence on Mexico's *mestizo* culture, which was already a fusion of Spanish and indigenous elements. The dance also reflects the traditions of the southwestern United States.

Lead-up activities and teaching suggestions are provided at the end of the dance directions.

Introduction: 4 microbeats

Formation: Partners in a double circle facing counterclockwise, skater's hold (see page 66 for more information). Directions given are for inside person.

Part I

Counterclockwise

FWD	FWD	FWD	TURN (½)	BWD	BWD	BWD	BWD
L	R	L	R	L	R	L	R

REPEAT, OPPOSITE DIRECTION

Beats 1–4	Walk 4 steps forward counterclockwise (on fourth step turn 180° to face clockwise).
5–8	Walk 4 steps backward counterclockwise.
9–16	Repeat Part I, beats 1–8, moving clockwise.

Keep R handhold with partner, release L hand with partner and take neighbor's hand; males are facing out of circle, females are facing into circle.

Note: Part I shown on the facing page is a simplification; the actual Part I follows:

Beats 1–4	Males walk L, R, L, R foot.
5	Step L foot sideward left (counterclockwise).
6	Step R foot crossing in back of L foot.
7	Step L foot sideward left.
8	Touch R foot next to L foot.
9–16	Repeat beats 1–8 in opposite direction beginning R foot (females use opposite side footwork on beats 1–16).

Part II

IN	TOUCH	OUT	TOUCH	TURN	TURN	TURN	TURN
L	**(R)**	**R**	**(L)**	**L**	**R**	**L**	**R**

IN	TOUCH	OUT	TOUCH	TURN	TURN	TURN	TURN
L	**(R)**	**R**	**(L)**	**L**	**R**	**L**	**R**

Beats 17–18 Step R foot into the space and touch L foot next to R foot.

19–20 Step L foot out of the space and touch R foot next to L foot.

21–24 Turn ½ using 4 steps, keeping R handhold with partner (you are now facing the opposite direction).

25–28 Repeat beats 17–20.

29–32 Keep holding neighbor's L hand and release partner's R hand; move in 4 steps to a position side by side with neighbor; start dance from beginning with new partner.

Lead-up Activities: First move counterclockwise 8 steps, then move clockwise 8 steps. Walk 4 steps FORWARD, turn 180° and walk BACKWARD 4 steps (individual tempo). Practice the above with a partner using skater's hold (partner beat).

Teaching Suggestions: Practice Part I with a partner (partner beat, then SAY & DO), and teach the simplification before attempting the actual dance. Have the students move into the formation for beats 17–24 — SAY "INTO the space, OUT of the space, TURN OUT of the space, your neighbor is your partner." Return to original partner and practice beats 17–32 until executed successfully. Practice the transition from beat 16 to beat 17. SAY & DO the entire dance and then add the music.

Skater's Hold

Name: ______________________________ Date: ______________

Trim the Tree

The holidays are coming and we need to decorate our Christmas tree! Color all the ornaments according to the directions on the right. If you have time, color the tree, too.

Color all the...

Eighth notes = Red
Quarter notes = Blue
Half notes = Orange
Dotted half notes = Gray
Whole notes = Purple
Eighth rests = Pink
Quarter rests = Light Blue
Half rests = Yellow
Whole rests = Red Violet

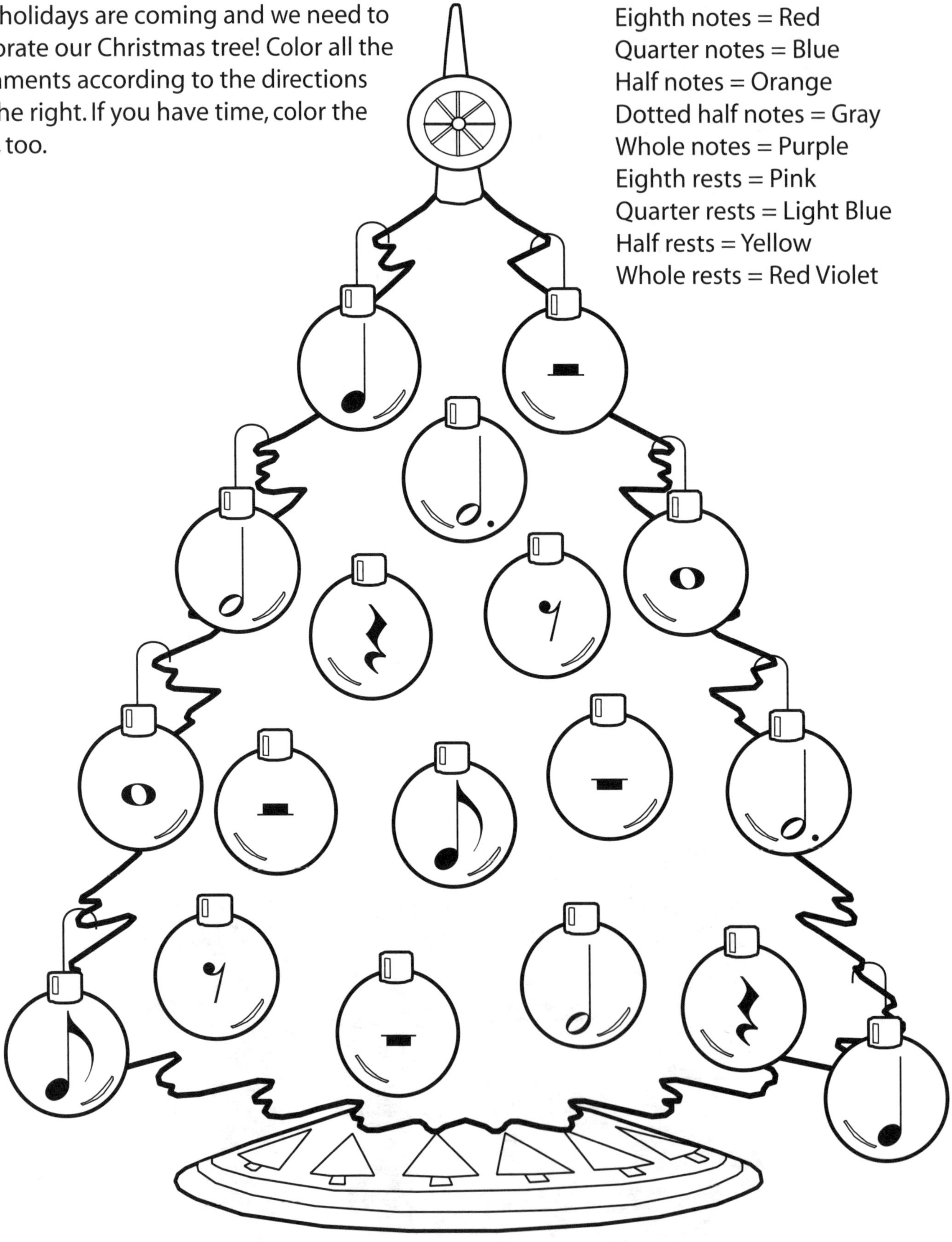

Name: ______________________________ Date: ______________

Nearly Nap Time

It's Festival of Sleep Day and our music teacher wants to take a nap, but she can't until all the instruments are put away. Help her by unscrambling the mixed-up instrument names below. When you're finished, draw a line from the instrument name to its picture. HINT: If you're having trouble unscrambling a name, work backwards from the pictures—figure out the name of each instrument pictured then see which of the scrambled words could be that instrument.

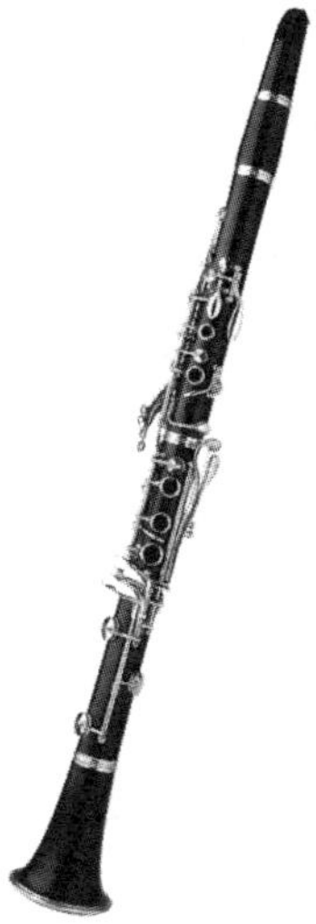

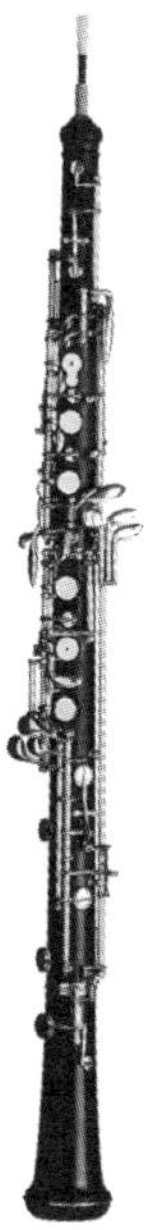

ATBU ______________________

BOEO ______________________

LAIOV ______________________

OOSSBAN ______________________

PAINTMI ______________________

PETTRUM ______________________

RAINTGLE ______________________

TENIRALC ______________________

TIRGAU ______________________

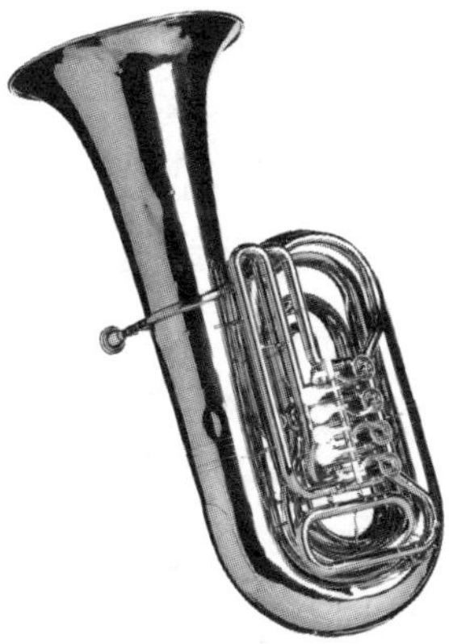

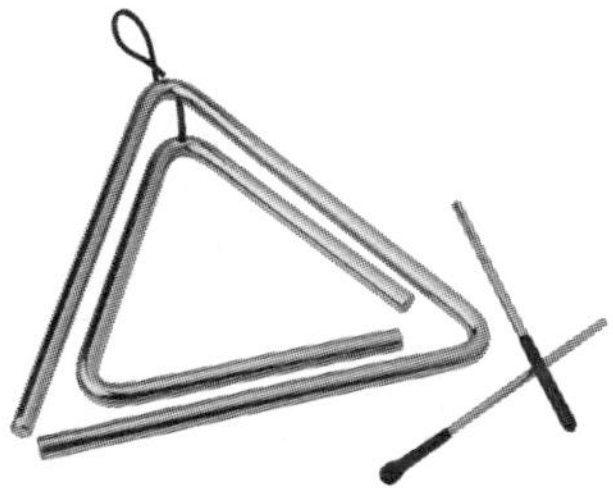

Name: ______________________________ Date: ______________

Melodic Twists and Turns

Have you ever seen ivy? It climbs up, then down, then goes straight across, then maybe down again, and back up. Melodies, or tunes, are like this too. The notes can move up or down by *steps*, to the note on the space or line right next door. They can also jump to a note farther away, which is called a *skip*. Notes may also repeat.

First, describe the movement from note to note in the melodies below. An example is given for you.

Example:

skip up | step down | step down | repeat | skip down | step up | step up

1.

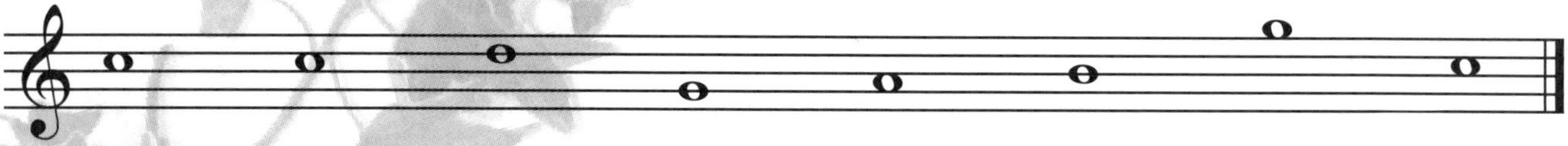

______ ______ ______ ______ ______ ______ ______

2.

______ ______ ______ ______ ______ ______ ______

Now, write a melody that fits each of the descriptions below. You may use any notes you wish, but you need to name each when you're finished, so be sure to use notes you know! Again, an example is given.

Example:

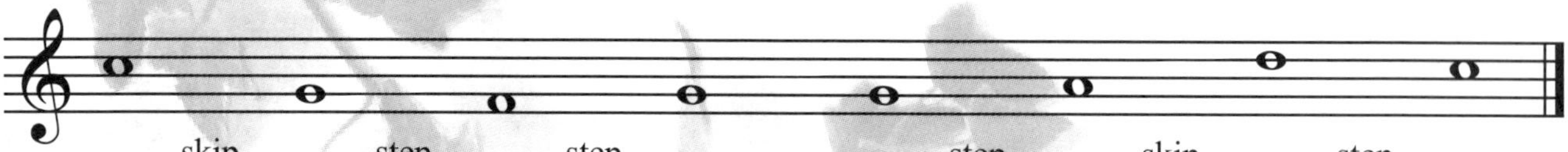

C skip down G step down F step up G repeat G step up A skip up C step down C

1.

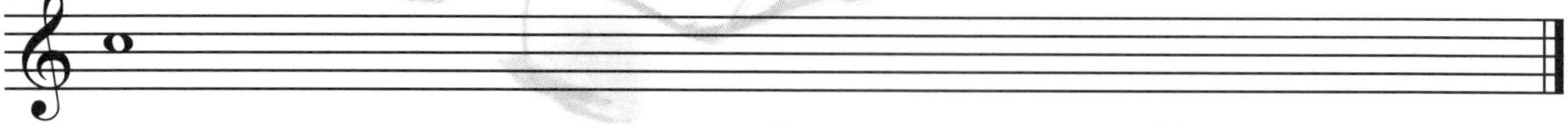

____ step up ____ step up ____ repeat ____ skip down ____ step down ____ skip up ____ repeat ____

2.

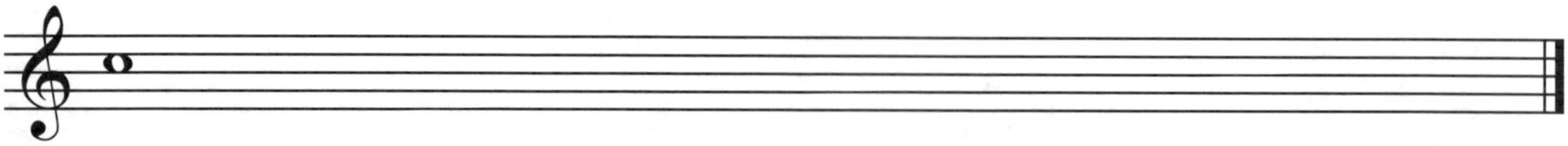

____ skip down ____ step up ____ skip up ____ repeat ____ step down ____ repeat ____ step up ____

Name: ______________________________ Date: ______________

WHAT'S THE PLAY?

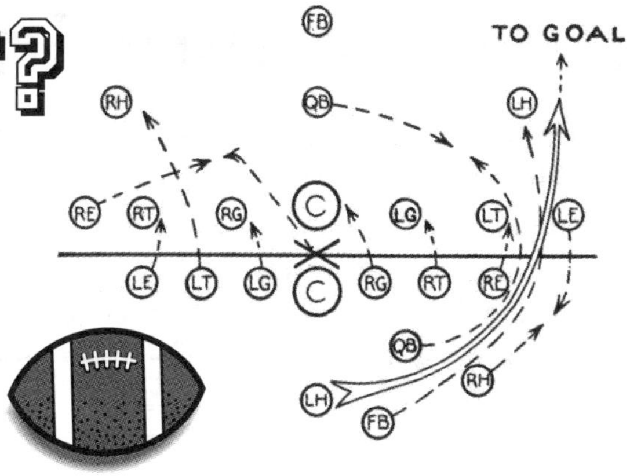

Our team is trying to get ready for the big game but all the "plays" are missing their time signatures. Help coach the team by adding the correct time signature to each of the examples below. Hint: Choose from these time signatures:

$\frac{4}{4}$ $\frac{3}{4}$ $\frac{2}{4}$ $\frac{6}{8}$

1 

2 

3 

4 

5 

6 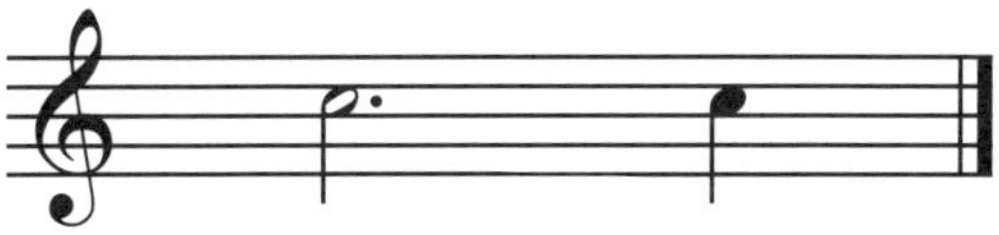

7 

8 

9 

10 

Name: ______________________________ Date: ______________

A Symphony in Pictures

When talking about classical music, people use the word *symphony* a lot. Sometimes, particularly in America, symphony is used to describe a large group of musicians who play classical music, as in "I went to the symphony last night. It was great!" But symphony is also the name of a type of piece. A symphony is a large work for orchestra. By "large," we mean that it is usually long, 35 minutes or more for some, and written for a lot of musicians. The word symphony even comes from a Greek word meaning, "a sounding together." Symphonies are also a large deal for composers; it's where they are really supposed to show off their stuff. And plenty have.

The first symphonies were written in the 1750s. The early Classical composer Joseph Haydn wrote more than 100 and was a big influence on Mozart, who wrote 41. Beethoven's nine symphonies are some of his finest work, as are Brahms's four, Mahler's 10, and Shostakovich's 15. (Composers today continue to write symphonies too, although many of them don't always follow the same "rules" as earlier composers.)

Symphonies usually have four *movements*, or sections. Typically, the first movement is fast. It is followed by a slow second movement, often in a minor key. The third movement is usually a dance in triple meter, like a minuet or scherzo. The fourth and final movement is fast (although usually not as fast the first). You can usually tell something's a symphony because it's named Symphony No. 1 or Symphony No. 4. Some composers, like Beethoven and Tchaikovsky, added descriptive titles to the names of their symphonies, like *Eroica* or *Pastorale*.

In the four boxes below, or on a separate sheet of paper that's been divided into four sections, draw your own symphony. You can use pictures, lines and shapes, anything that, to you, represents the form of a symphony. Don't forget to title your symphony when you're finished.

Getting a Handel on *Messiah*

The second-most-famous Baroque composer (Handel's bad luck for composing in the same period as one of the greatest masters of all time, J.S. Bach), George Frideric Handel (George FREE-der-ich HAHN-dul) was one of the first composers who was able to make a living solely as a composer. Born in Germany in 1685, Handel was trained as an organist and worked as a choir master there before moving to London, England, when he was 25. Handel loved England and stayed there for the rest of his life, even changing the spelling of his name from the German, Georg Frederich Händel to the English, George Frideric Handel.

In his time, classical music was the popular entertainment, so Handel was treated like today's pop stars. All the royalty in England wanted him to write pieces for them, and they invited him to all their parties. They, along with all of high society, also turned out to hear his latest opera. Although he wrote a lot of instrumental music and vocal solos, Handel's first musical love was opera. He wrote more than 40 of them, but unfortunately the kind of operas that he liked to write—more serious operas in an Italian style called *opera seria*—were becoming less and less popular with the English people. Comic operas with lighter, less serious (and sometimes crude) stories and music were taking over, but Handel wasn't willing to write this kind of opera. Problem was, Handel had become accustomed to living the rock-star life, and composing was his only job. He needed a hit show, and quick.

While recovering from an illness, Handel had an idea—a new way to write the more serious music that he liked, yet in a way that people would like—*oratorios*. Oratorios are extended choral works about a religious subject that have an orchestral accompaniment. They are like operas in that they tell a story with song and there are characters, but unlike opera, the performers don't wear costumes and they don't act out the story. Also appealing to Handel was the fact that the music could be more serious (since it was about Biblical stories), yet it would appeal to the people because of their strong connection to the traditional English church music.

Good news for Handel (and for all fans of classical music)—people loved his oratorios. Without a doubt, the most beloved of them is *Messiah*. (Not only popular, many scholars consider it his best work, period). *Messiah* was written and premiered in Dublin, Ireland, in 1742 to raise funds for an orphanage. Believe it or not, Handel wrote the entire work, which is almost three hours long, in just 24 days, orchestra parts included. *Messiah* includes one of the most recognizable pieces of classical music—*Hallelujah Chorus*. Although we hear *Messiah* a lot at Christmas time, Handel didn't write it as a Christmas piece (really, only Part I is about Christmas). In fact, the tradition of performing it at Christmas time is entirely a North American one. Of the 36 performances Handel conducted or oversaw, none were at Christmas.

Handel died in 1759. Commemorated during his lifetime with a life-size marble sculpture, he was also honored in death with a burial in Westminster Abbey. Others luminaries buried there include Mary, Queen of Scots, Elizabeth I, Charles Dickens, Rudyard Kipling, and Sir Isaac Newton. Interestingly, the marker there indicates that Handel was born in 1684. Embarrassing typo? No. Turns out that when he was born, England's calendar year started in March; since he was born in February, it was still considered 1684.

Answer Keys

Page 74

Trim the Tree

Ornaments should be colored as follows:

♪ – Red

♩ – Blue

𝅗𝅥 – Orange

𝅗𝅥. – Gray

𝅝 – Purple

𝄾 – Pink

𝄽 – Light Blue

𝄼 – Yellow

𝄻 – Red Violet

Page 75

Nearly Nap Time

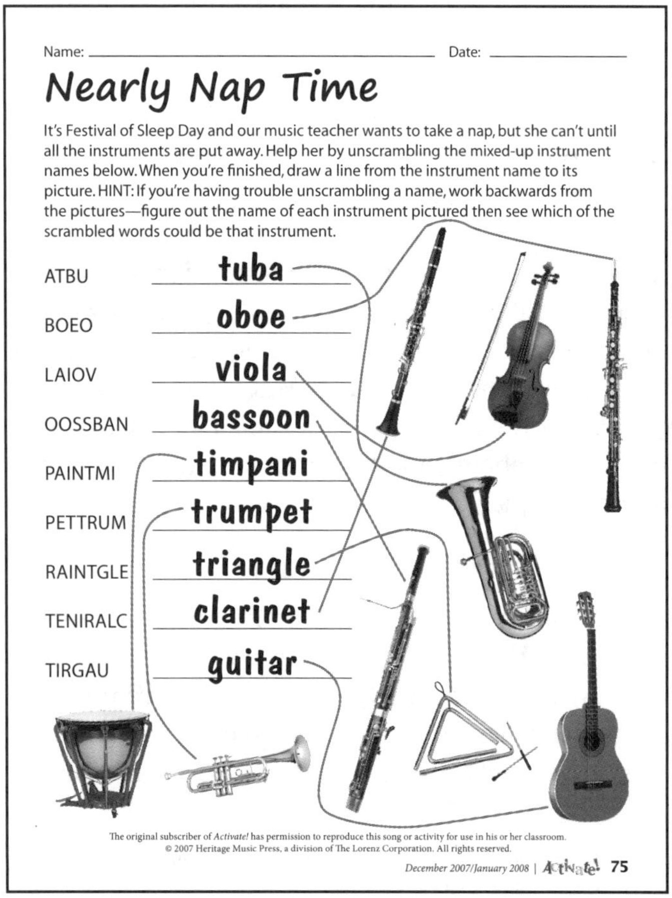

Name: ______ Date: ______

Nearly Nap Time

It's Festival of Sleep Day and our music teacher wants to take a nap, but she can't until all the instruments are put away. Help her by unscrambling the mixed-up instrument names below. When you're finished, draw a line from the instrument name to its picture. HINT: If you're having trouble unscrambling a name, work backwards from the pictures—figure out the name of each instrument pictured then see which of the scrambled words could be that instrument.

ATBU tuba
BOEO oboe
LAIOV viola
OOSSBAN bassoon
PAINTMI timpani
PETTRUM trumpet
RAINTGLE triangle
TENIRALC clarinet
TIRGAU guitar

The original subscriber of *Activate!* has permission to reproduce this song or activity for use in his or her classroom.
© 2007 Heritage Music Press, a division of The Lorenz Corporation. All rights reserved.

December 2007/January 2008 | Activate! 75

Page 76

Melodic Twists and Turn

1. Repeat, Step Up, Skip Down, Step Up, Step Up, Skip Up, Skip Down
2. Skip Down, Step Up, Repeat, Skip Down, Skip Down, Skip Up, Skip Down

(There are numerous correct answers for the second set of exercises.)

Page 77

What's the Play?

1. $\frac{4}{4}$
2. $\frac{3}{4}$
3. $\frac{6}{8}$
4. $\frac{3}{4}$
5. $\frac{2}{4}$
6. $\frac{4}{4}$
7. $\frac{2}{4}$
8. $\frac{6}{8}$
9. $\frac{3}{4}$
10. $\frac{4}{4}$